GREAT EXPECTATIONS

It is a great human weakness to wish to be the same as our friends. If they are rich, we wish to be rich. If they are poor, then we don't mind being equally poor. We are not ashamed of being stupid, we are only ashamed of being more stupid than our friends. It is a matter of comparison.

It is also a matter of expectation. We don't miss things that we never expected to have. We are not disappointed at being poor if we never expected to be rich.

Pip is poor and uneducated, but so are his friends. For them, this is normal; this is what life is like. But when Pip is told that he has "great expectations", he becomes dissatisfied. He is ashamed of his friends, and he is ashamed of himself. His expectations are in danger of ruining his life.

Great Expectations

Stage 5 (1800 headwords)

Series Editor: Jennifer Bassett
Founder Editor: Tricia Hedge
Activities Editors: Jennifer Bassett and Alison Baxter

American Edition: Daphne Mackey, University of Washington

CHARLES DICKENS

Great Expectations

Retold by
Clare West

OXFORD UNIVERSITY PRESS

OXFORD
UNIVERSITY PRESS

Great Clarendon Street, Oxford OX2 6DP

Oxford University Press is a department of the University of Oxford.
It furthers the University's objective of excellence in research, scholarship,
and education by publishing worldwide in

Oxford New York

Auckland Cape Town Dar es Salaam Hong Kong Karachi
Kuala Lumpur Madrid Melbourne Mexico City Nairobi
New Delhi Shanghai Taipei Toronto

With offices in

Argentina Austria Brazil Chile Czech Republic France Greece
Guatemala Hungary Italy Japan Poland Portugal Singapore
South Korea Switzerland Thailand Turkey Ukraine Vietnam

OXFORD and OXFORD ENGLISH are registered trade marks of
Oxford University Press in the UK and in certain other countries

First published in Oxford Bookworms 1992

10 12 14 15 13 11

ISBN 978 0 19 423760 4

Printed in China

ACKNOWLEDGMENTS

Illustrated by: Susan Scott

CONTENTS

PEOPLE IN THIS STORY

Pip
Joe Gargery, *the village blacksmith*
Mrs. Joe Gargery, *Joe's wife and Pip's sister*
Mr. Pumblechook, *Joe's uncle*
Mr. Wopsle, *the church clerk, later an actor*
Biddy, *Mr. Wopsle's young cousin*
Orlick, *a blacksmith working for Joe Gargery*
Abel Magwitch, *a convict*
Compeyson, *also a convict*
Miss Havisham, *a rich lady*
Estella, *adopted by Miss Havisham*
Matthew Pocket, *Miss Havisham's cousin*
Herbert Pocket, *his son*
Clara, *engaged to Herbert*
Startop, *a young gentleman*
Bentley Drummle, *a young gentleman*
Mr. Jaggers, *a London lawyer*
Molly, *Mr. Jaggers' housekeeper*
Mr. Wemmick, *Mr. Jaggers' clerk*
The aged parent (the Aged), *Wemmick's father*
Miss Skiffins, *engaged to Wemmick*

1

Pip Meets a Stranger

My first name was Philip, but when I was a small child I could only manage to say Pip. So Pip was what everybody called me. I lived in a small village in Essex with my sister, who was over twenty years older than me, and who was married to Joe Gargery, the village blacksmith. My parents had died when I was a baby, so I could not remember them at all, but quite often I used to visit the churchyard, about a mile from the village, to look at their names on their gravestones.

My first memory is of sitting on a gravestone in that churchyard one cold, gray, December afternoon, looking out at the dark, flat, wild marshes divided by the black line of the River Thames and listening to the rushing sound of the sea in the distance.

"Don't say a word!" cried a terrible voice, as a man jumped up from among the graves and caught hold of me. "If you shout, I'll cut your throat!" He was a big man, dressed all in gray, with an iron chain on his leg. His clothes were wet and torn. He looked exhausted, and hungry, and very fierce. I had never been so frightened in my whole life.

"Oh! Don't cut my throat, sir!" I begged in terror.

"Tell me your name, boy! Quick!" he said, still holding me. "And show me where you live!"

"My name's Pip, sir. And I live in the village over there."

He picked me up and turned me upside-down. Nothing fell out of my pocket except a piece of old bread. He ate it in two bites, like a dog, and put me back on the gravestone.

"So where are your father and mother?" he asked.

"There, sir," I answered, pointing to their graves.

"What!" he cried, and he was about to run, when he saw where I was pointing. "Oh!" he said. "I see. They're dead. Well, who do you live with, if I let you live, which I haven't decided yet?"

"With my sister, sir, wife of Joe Gargery, the blacksmith."

"Blacksmith, you say?" And he looked down at his leg. Then he held me by both arms and stared fiercely down into my eyes.

"Now look here. You bring me a file. You know what that is? And you bring me some food. If you don't, or if you tell anyone about me, I'll cut your heart out."

"I promise I'll do it, sir," I answered. I was badly frightened, and my whole body was trembling.

"You see," he continued, smiling unpleasantly, "I travel with a young man, a friend of mine, who roasts boys' hearts and eats them. He'll find you, wherever you are, and he'll have your heart. So bring the file and the food to that wooden shelter over there, early tomorrow morning, if you want to keep your heart, that is. Remember, you promised!"

I watched him turn and walk with difficulty across the marshes, the chain hanging clumsily around his leg. Then I ran home as fast as I could.

My sister, Mrs. Joe Gargery, was very proud of the fact that she had brought me up "by hand." Nobody explained to me what this meant, and because she had a hard and heavy hand, which she used freely on her husband as well as me, I supposed that Joe and I were both brought up by hand. She was not a beautiful woman, being tall and thin, with black hair and eyes and a very red face. She clearly felt that Joe and I caused her a lot of trouble, and she frequently complained about it. Joe, on the other hand, was a gentle, kind man with fair hair and weak blue eyes, who quietly accepted her scolding.

Because Joe and I were in the same position of being scolded by Mrs. Joe, we were good friends, and Joe protected me from her anger whenever he could. So when I ran breathless into the kitchen, he gave me a friendly warning. "She's out looking for you, Pip! And she's got the stick with her!" This stick had been used so often for beating me that it was now quite smooth.

Just then Mrs. Joe rushed in.

"Where have you been, you young monkey?" she shouted. I jumped behind Joe to avoid being hit with the stick.

"Only to the churchyard," I whispered, starting to cry.

"Churchyard! If I hadn't brought you up, you'd be in the churchyard with our parents. You'll send *me* to the churchyard one day! Now let me get your supper ready, both of you!"

For the rest of the evening, I thought of nothing but the stranger on the marshes. Sometimes, as the wind blew around the house, I imagined I heard his voice outside, and I thought with horror of the young man who ate boys' hearts.

Just before I went to bed, we heard the sound of a big gun on the marshes. "Was that a gun, Joe?" I asked.

"Ah!" said Joe. "Another convict's escaped. One got away last night. They always fire the gun when one escapes."

"Who fires the gun?" I asked. Joe shook his head to warn me.

"Too many questions," frowned my sister. "If you must know it's the men in the prison ships who fire the gun."

"I wonder who is put into prison ships, and why?" I asked, in a general way, quietly desperate to know the answer.

This was too much for Mrs. Joe. "Listen, my boy, I didn't bring you up by hand to annoy people to death! There are ships on the river which are used as prisons. People who steal and murder are put in the prison ships, and they stay there for years sometimes. And they always begin their life of crime by asking too many questions! Now, go to bed!"

I could not sleep at all that night. I was in terror of the young man who wanted my heart, I was in terror of the man with the iron chain, and I was in terror of my sister, who would soon discover I had stolen her food. As soon as there was a little light in the sky outside my window, I got up and went quietly down to the kitchen. I stole some bread, cheese, and a big meat pie, hoping that, as there was a lot of food ready for Christmas, nobody would notice what was missing. I did not dare take the whole brandy bottle, so I poured some into a smaller bottle to take away with me. Then I filled up the brandy bottle with what I thought was water from a big brown bottle. I took a file from Joe's box of tools and ran out on to the dark marshes.

The mist was so thick that I could not see anything. Although I knew my way to the shelter very well, I almost got lost this time. I was near it when I saw a man sitting on the ground, half asleep. I went up and touched his shoulder. He jumped up, and it was the wrong man! He was dressed in gray, too, and had an iron chain on his leg. He ran away into the mist.

"It's the young man!" I thought, feeling a pain in my heart.

When I arrived at the shelter, I found the right man. He looked so cold and hungry that I felt sorry for him. Trembling violently, he swallowed the brandy and ate the food like a hunted animal, looking around him all the time for danger.

"You're sure you didn't tell anyone? Or bring anyone?"

"No, sir. I'm glad you're enjoying the food, sir."

"Thank you, my boy. You've been good to a poor man."

"But I'm afraid there won't be any left for *him*."

"Him? Who's that?" My friend stopped in the middle of eating.

"The young man who travels with you."

"Oh, him!" he replied, smiling. "*He* doesn't want any food."

"I thought he looked rather hungry," I answered.

He stared at me in great surprise. "Looked? When?"

"Just now, over there. I found him half asleep, and I thought it was you. He was dressed like you, and—" I was anxious to express this politely "—he had the same reason for wanting to borrow a file."

"Then I *did* hear them fire the gun last night! You know, boy, when you're on the marsh alone at night, you imagine all kinds of things, voices calling, guns firing, soldiers marching! But show me where this man went. I'll find him, and I'll finish with him! I'll smash his face! Give me the file first."

I was afraid of him now that he was angry again.

"I'm sorry, I must go home now," I said. He did not seem to hear, so I left him bending over his leg and filing away at his iron chain like a madman. Halfway home I stopped in the mist to listen, and I could still hear the sound of the file.

2

Catching a Convict

All that morning I was frightened that my sister would discover that I had stolen from her, but luckily she was so busy cleaning the house and roasting the chickens for our Christmas lunch that she did not notice that I had been out or that any food was missing. At half-past one our two guests arrived. Mr. Wopsle, the church clerk, had a large nose and a shining, bald forehead. Mr. Pumblechook, who had a shop in the nearest town, was a fat, middle-aged man with a mouth like a fish, and staring eyes. He was really Joe's uncle, but it was Mrs. Joe who called him uncle. Every Christmas Day he arrived with two bottles of wine, handing them proudly to my sister.

"Oh Uncle Pumblechook! This is kind!" she always replied.

"It's no more than you deserve," was the answer every time.

Sitting at table with these guests, I would have felt uncomfortable even if I hadn't robbed my sister. Not only was Pumblechook's elbow in my eye, but I wasn't allowed to speak, and they gave me the worst pieces of meat. Even the chickens must have been ashamed of those parts of their bodies when they were alive. And worse than that, the adults never left me in peace.

"Before we eat, let us thank God for the food in front of us," said Mr. Wopsle, in the deep voice he used in church.

"Do you hear that?" whispered my sister to me. "Be grateful!"

"Especially," said Mr. Pumblechook firmly, "be grateful, boy, to those who brought you up by hand."

"Why are the young never grateful?" wondered Mr. Wopsle sadly.

"Their characters are naturally bad," answered Mr. Pumblechook, and all three looked unpleasantly at me.

When there were guests, Joe's position was even lower than usual (if that was possible), but he always tried to help me if he could. Sometimes he comforted me by giving me extra gravy. He did that now.

"Just imagine, boy," said Mr. Pumblechook, "if your sister hadn't brought you up—"

"You listen to this," said my sister to me crossly.

"If, as I say, she hadn't spent her life looking after you, where would you be now?"

Joe offered me more gravy.

"He was a lot of trouble to you, madam," Mr. Wopsle said sympathetically to my sister.

"Trouble?" she cried. "Trouble?" And then she started on a list of all my illnesses, accidents, and crimes while everybody except Joe looked at me with disgust. Joe added more gravy to the meat swimming on my plate, and I wanted to pull Mr. Wopsle's nose.

In the end Mrs. Joe stopped for breath and said to Mr. Pumblechook, "Have a little brandy, uncle. There is a bottle already open."

It had happened at last! Now she would discover I had stolen some brandy and put water in the bottle. Mr. Pumblechook held his glass up to the light, smiled importantly at it, and drank it. When, immediately afterwards, he jumped up and began to rush around the room in a strange wild dance, we all stared at him in great surprise. Was he mad? I wondered if I had murdered him, but if so, how? At last he threw himself gasping into a chair, crying "Medicine!" Then I understood. Instead of filling up the brandy bottle with water, I had put Mrs. Joe's strongest and most unpleasant medicine in by mistake. That was what the big brown bottle contained.

"But how could my medicine get into a brandy bottle?" asked my sister. Fortunately she had no time to find the answer, as Mr. Pumblechook was calling for a hot rum to remove the taste of the medicine. "And now," she said, when the fat man was calmer, "you must all try Uncle Pumblechook's present to us! A really delicious meat pie!"

"That's right, Mrs. Joe!" said Mr. Pumblechook, looking more cheerful now. "Bring in the pie!"

"You shall have some, Pip," said Joe kindly.

I knew what would happen next. I could not sit there any longer. I jumped down from the table and ran out of the room.

But at the front door I ran straight into a group of soldiers. Mrs. Joe was saying as she came out of the kitchen, "The pie—has—gone!" but stopped when she saw the soldiers.

"Excuse me, ladies and gentlemen," said the officer in charge.

He jumped up and began to rush around the room in a strange wild dance.

"I'm here in the King's name, and I want the blacksmith."

"And why do you want him?" said my sister crossly.

"Madam," replied the officer politely, "speaking for myself, I'd like the pleasure of meeting his fine wife. Speaking for the King, I'd like him to repair these handcuffs."

"Ah, very good, very good!" said Mr. Pumblechook, clapping.

The soldiers waited in the kitchen while Joe lit the forge fire and started work. I began to feel better now that everyone had forgotten the missing pie.

"How far are we from the marshes?" asked the officer.

"About a mile," replied Mrs. Joe.

"That's good. We'll catch them before it's dark."

"Convicts, officer?" asked Mr. Wopsle.

"Yes, two escaped convicts out on the marshes. Has anyone here seen them?"

The others all shook their heads. Nobody asked me. When the handcuffs were ready, Joe suggested we should go with the soldiers, and as Mrs. Joe was curious to know what happened, she agreed. So Joe, Mr. Wopsle, and I walked behind the men through the village and out on to the marshes.

"I hope we don't find those poor men, Joe," I whispered.

"I hope not either, Pip," he whispered back. It was cold, with an east wind blowing from the sea, and it was getting dark.

Suddenly we all stopped. We heard shouts in the distance.

"This way! Run!" the officer ordered, and we all rushed in that direction. The shouts became clearer. "Murder!" "Escaped convict!" "Help!" At last we discovered two men fighting each other. One was my convict, and the other was the man who had run away when I had seen him near the shelter. Somehow the soldiers held the men apart and put the handcuffs on them.

"Here he is—I'm holding him for you!" shouted my convict.

"Officer, he tried to murder me!" cried the other man. His

face was bleeding, and he was clearly very frightened.

"Murder him! No," said the first, "that would be too easy. I want him to suffer more, back on the prison ship. He's lying, as he did at our trial! You can't trust Compeyson!"

Just then he noticed me for the first time. I shook my head at him to show that I had not wanted the soldiers to find him. He stared at me, but I did not know if he understood or not.

The prisoners were taken to the riverside, where a boat was waiting to take them on to the prison ship. Just as he was about to leave, my convict said, "Officer, after my escape, I stole some food from the blacksmith's house. Bread, cheese, brandy, and a meat pie. I'm sorry I ate your pie, blacksmith."

"I'm glad you did," replied Joe kindly. "We don't know why you're a convict, but we wouldn't want you to die of hunger."

The man rubbed his eyes with the back of his dirty hand. We watched the small boat carry him out to the middle of the river, where the great black prison ship stood high out of the water, held by its rusty chains. He disappeared into the ship, and I thought that was the last I had seen of him.

3

An Opportunity for Pip

I always knew I would be apprenticed to Joe as soon as I was old enough, and so I used to spend most of the day helping him in the forge. However, I also attended the village evening school, which was organized by an ancient relation of Mr. Wopsle's. Her teaching mostly consisted of falling asleep while we children fought each other, but Mr. Wopsle's young cousin, Biddy, tried to keep us under control and teach us to read, write, and count. Mr. Wopsle "examined" us every three months. In fact, he did not ask us any questions at all, but read aloud from Shakespeare, waving his arms dramatically and enjoying the sound of his own voice.

One night, about a year after the escaped convicts had been caught, I was sitting by the kitchen fire, writing a letter to Joe. I didn't need to, because he was sitting right next to me, but I wanted to practice my writing. After an hour or two of hard work, I passed this letter to him.

"mY deAr JOe I hopE yOu Are welL sOon i Can teAcH yoU wHat I hAve leaRned WHat fuN JoE LovE PiP"

"Pip, old boy!" cried Joe, opening his kind blue eyes very wide. "What a lot you've learned! Here's a J and an O, that's for Joe, isn't it, Pip?"

I wondered whether I would have to teach Joe from the beginning, so I asked, "How do you write Gargery, Joe?"

"*I* don't write it at all," said Joe. "But, you know, I *am* fond of reading. Give me a good book or newspaper and a good fire, and I ask no more. Well! When you come to a J and an O, how interesting reading is!"

"Didn't you ever go to school, Joe, when you were young?"

"No, Pip. You see, my father drank a lot, and when he drank, he used to hit my mother, and me too, sometimes. So she and I ran away from him several times. And she used to say, 'Now, Joe, you can go to school.' But my father had such a good heart that he didn't want to be without us. So he always came to find us, took us home, and hit us. So you see, Pip, I never learned much."

"Poor Joe!"

"But remember, Pip, my father had a good heart."

I wondered about that, but said nothing.

"He let me become a blacksmith, which was his job too, only he never worked at it. I earned the money for the family until he died. And listen to this, Pip. I wanted to put this on his gravestone:

Whatever the fault he had from the start,

Remember, reader, he had a good heart."

"Did you invent that yourself, Joe?" I asked, surprised.

"I did," said Joe proudly. "It came to me in a moment. From my own head. But, Pip, sad to say, there wasn't enough money for the gravestone. My poor mother needed it. In bad health, she was. She died soon after. Found peace at last." Joe's blue eyes were watery. "I was lonely then, and I met your sister. Now, Pip," Joe looked firmly at me because he knew I was not going to agree with him, "your sister is a fine woman!"

I could think of nothing better to say than "I'm glad you think so, Joe."

"So am I," said Joe. "I'm glad *I* think so. Very kind of her, bringing you up by hand. Such a tiny baby you were! So when I offered to marry your sister, I said, 'And bring the poor little child to live with us. There's room for him at the forge!' "

I put my arms around Joe's neck and cried into his shirt.

"Don't cry, old boy!" he said. "Always the best of friends, you and me!" As I dried my tears, he continued, "So here we are, Pip! Now if you teach me a bit (and I warn you now that I'm very stupid), Mrs. Joe must never know. And why? Because she likes to be—in charge—you know—giving the orders."

"Joe," I asked, "why don't you ever rebel?"

"Well," said Joe, "to start with, your sister's clever. And I'm not. And another thing, and this is serious, old boy, when I think of my poor mother's hard life, I'm afraid of not behaving right to a woman. So I'd much rather seem a bit weak with Mrs. Joe than shout at her, or hurt her, or hit her. I'm just sorry she scolds you as well, Pip, and hits you with the stick. I wish I could take all the scolding myself. But there it is, Pip."

Just then we heard the sound of a horse on the road. Mrs. Joe and Uncle Pumblechook were returning from the market. The carriage arrived, and in a rush of cold air, they were in the kitchen.

"Now," said Mrs. Joe, excitedly throwing off her cloak, "if this boy isn't grateful tonight, he never will be!"

"She's offering the boy a great opportunity," agreed Pumblechook. Trying to look grateful, I looked at Joe, making the word "She?" with my lips. He clearly did not know either.

"You were speaking of a she?" he said politely to them.

"She is a she, I suppose," Mrs. Joe replied crossly. "Unless you call Miss Havisham a he. And even *you* wouldn't do that."

"The rich Miss Havisham, who lives all alone in the big house in town?" asked Joe.

"There aren't any other Miss Havishams that I know of! She wants a boy to go and play there. She asked Uncle Pumblechook if he knew of anyone. And Uncle Pumblechook, thinking of us as he always does, suggested this boy. And what's more, Uncle Pumblechook, realizing that this boy's fortune may be made by going to Miss Havisham's, has offered to take him into town tonight in his carriage, let him sleep in his own house, and deliver him tomorrow to Miss Havisham's. And just look!" she cried, catching hold of me. "Look at the dirt on this boy!"

I was washed from top to toe in Mrs. Joe's usual violent manner and handed over, in my tightest Sunday clothes, to Mr. Pumblechook. In the carriage taking me into town, I cried a little. I had never been away from Joe before, and I had no idea what was going to happen to me at Miss Havisham's.

Mr. Pumblechook seemed to agree with my sister that I should be punished as much as possible, even when eating, and so for breakfast next morning he gave me a large piece of bread with very little butter and a cup of warm water with very little milk, and insisted on checking my learning.

"What's seven and thirteen, boy?" He continued testing me all through breakfast. "And nine? And eleven?"

So I was glad to arrive at Miss Havisham's house at about ten o'clock. It was a large house, made of old stone, with iron bars on the windows. We rang the bell and waited at the gate. Even then Mr. Pumblechook said, "And fourteen?" but I pretended not to hear him. Then a young lady came to open the gate and let me in. Mr. Pumblechook was following me when she stopped him.

"Do you wish to see Miss Havisham?" she asked.

"If Miss Havisham wishes to see me," answered Mr. Pumblechook, a little confused.

"Ah!" said the girl, "but you see, she doesn't."

Mr. Pumblechook dared not protest, but he whispered angrily to me before he turned away, "Boy! Behave well here, and remember those who brought you up by hand!" I thought he would come back and call through the gate, "And sixteen?" but he did not.

The young lady took me through the untidy garden to the house. Although she called me "boy," she was the same age as me, but she seemed much older than me. She was beautiful and as proud as a queen. We went through many dark passages until we reached a door, where she left me, taking her candle with her.

I knocked at the door and was told to enter. I found myself in a large room, where the curtains were closed to allow no daylight in and the candles were lit. In the center of the room,

The strangest lady I have ever seen.

sitting at a table, was the strangest lady I have ever seen or shall ever see. She was wearing a wedding dress made of rich material. She had a bride's flowers in her hair, but her hair was white. There were suitcases full of dresses and jewels around her, ready for a journey. She only had one white shoe on. Then I realized that over the years the white wedding dress had become yellow, the flowers in her hair had died, and the bride inside the dress had grown old. Everything in the room was ancient and dying. The only brightness in the room was in her dark old eyes, which stared at me.

"Who are you?" said the lady at the table.

"Pip, madam. Mr. Pumblechook's boy. Come—to play."

"Come close. Let me look at you." As I stood in front of her, I noticed that her watch and a clock in the room had both stopped at twenty minutes to nine.

"You aren't afraid of a woman who has never seen the sun since you were born?" asked Miss Havisham.

I am sorry to say I told a huge lie by saying, "No."

"Do you know what this is?" she asked, putting her hand on her left side.

"Yes, madam." It made me think of my convict's traveling companion. "Your heart, madam," I added.

"My heart! Broken!" she cried almost proudly, with a strange smile. Then she said, "I am tired. I want to see something different. Play."

No order could be more difficult to obey in that house and that room. I was desperate enough to consider rushing around the table pretending to be Pumblechook's carriage, but I could not make myself do it, and I just stood there helplessly.

"I'm very sorry, madam," I said. "My sister will be very angry with me if you complain, but I can't play just now. Everything is so strange, and new, and sad . . ." I stopped, afraid to say more. Miss Havisham looked down at her dress, and then at her face in the mirror on the table.

"So strange to him, so well-known to me," she whispered. "So new to him, so old to me. And so sad to us both! Call Estella!"

When Estella finally came, with her candle, along the dark passage, Miss Havisham picked up a jewel from her table and put it in Estella's hair. "Very pretty, my dear. It will be yours one day. Now let me see you play cards with this boy."

"With this boy! But he's a common working boy!"

I thought I heard Miss Havisham whisper, "Well! You can break his heart!" She sat, like a dead body ready for the grave, watching us play cards in the candle-light. I almost wondered if she was afraid that daylight would turn her into dust.

"What coarse hands this boy has! And what thick boots!" cried Estella in disgust before we had finished our first game. I was suddenly aware that what she said was true.

"What do you think of her?" whispered Miss Havisham to me.

"I think she's very proud," I whispered back.

"Anything else?"

"I think she's very pretty."

"Anything else?"

"I think she's very rude. And—and I'd like to go home."

"And never see her again although she's so pretty?"

"I don't know. I'd—I'd like to go home now."

Miss Havisham smiled. "You can go home. Come again in six days' time. Estella, give him some food. Go, Pip."

And so I found myself back in the overgrown garden in the bright daylight. Estella put some bread and meat down on the ground for me, like a dog. I was so offended by her behavior towards me that tears came to my eyes. As soon as she saw this, she gave a delighted laugh and pushed me out of the gate. I walked the four miles home to the forge, thinking about all I had seen. As I looked sadly at my hands and boots, I remembered that I was only a common working boy and wished I could be different.

My sister was curious to know all the details of my visit and kept asking me question after question. Somehow I felt I could not, or did not want to, explain about Miss Havisham and her strange house. I knew my sister would not understand. And the worst of it was that old fool Pumblechook arrived at tea-time to ask more questions. Just looking at his fishy staring eyes and open mouth made me want to keep silent.

"Leave this boy to me, madam," he told Mrs. Joe. "I'll make him concentrate. Now, boy, what's forty-three and seventy-two?"

"I don't know," I said. I didn't care, either.

"Is it eighty-five, for example?" he joked.

"Yes!" I answered, although I knew it wasn't. My sister hit me hard on the head.

"Boy!" he continued. "Describe Miss Havisham."

"Very tall and dark," I said, lying.

"Is she, uncle?" asked my sister eagerly.

"Oh yes," answered Mr. Pumblechook. So I knew immediately that he had never seen her. "This is the way to get information from this boy," he added quietly to Mrs. Joe.

"How well you make him obey you, uncle!" said Mrs. Joe.

"Now, boy! What was she doing when you arrived?"

"She was sitting in a black carriage," I replied.

Mr. Pumblechook and Mrs. Joe stared at each other. "In a black carriage?" they repeated.

"Yes," I said, becoming more confident. "And Miss Estella, her niece, I think, handed in gold plates with cake and wine through the windows."

"Was anybody else there?" asked Mr. Pumblechook.

"Four dogs, huge ones. They ate meat out of a silver basket."

"Where was this carriage, boy?"

"In her room. But there weren't any horses."

"Can this be possible, uncle?" asked Mrs. Joe.

"She's a strange woman, madam. It's quite possible. What did you play at, boy?"

"We played with flags," I answered. What lies I was telling! "Estella waved a blue one, I had a red one, and Miss Havisham waved one with little gold stars on, out of the carriage window."

Fortunately, they asked no more questions and were still discussing the wonderful things I had seen when Joe came in from the forge. When I saw his blue eyes open wide in surprise, I felt very sorry I had lied, and that evening, as soon as I found Joe alone for a moment, I confessed to him that I had lied about my visit to Miss Havisham.

"Is none of it true, Pip?" he asked, shocked. "No black

carriage? But at least there were dogs, weren't there, Pip? No? Not even one dog?"

"No, Joe, I'm sorry."

"Pip, old boy!" His kind face looked very unhappy. "If you tell lies, where do you think you'll go when you die?"

"I know, Joe, it's terrible. I don't know what happened. Oh I wish I didn't have such thick boots and such coarse hands! I'm so miserable, Joe. That beautiful young lady at Miss Havisham's said I was common. And I know I am! Somehow that made me tell lies."

"One thing to remember, Pip," said Joe, lighting his pipe slowly, "is that lies are always wrong. You can't stop being common by telling lies. That's not the way to do it. And you're learning all the time, Pip! Look at that letter you wrote me last night! Even the King had to start learning at the beginning, didn't he? That reminds me, any flags at Miss Havisham's? No? That's a pity. Look here, Pip, this is a true friend speaking to you. Take my advice. No more lies, live well, and die happy."

Encouraged by Joe's honest words, I went to bed, but I couldn't stop myself thinking that Estella would consider Joe's boots too thick, his hands too coarse, and our whole family common. That was a day I shall never forget.

4

A Present from a Stranger

I desperately wanted to be accepted by Estella. I realized I could never become well-educated just by attending old Mrs. Wopsle's evening school, so I asked Mr. Wopsle's cousin

Biddy to teach me everything she knew. She helped me as much as she could, but I knew it would take a long time to reach Estella's level.

One evening I went to get Joe from the village pub, where my sister sometimes allowed him to smoke his pipe and have a beer. Mr. Wopsle and Joe were sitting with a stranger, a man I'd never seen before. One of his eyes was half closed, and he wore a big hat which covered most of his head. He suddenly looked interested when I arrived, and he rubbed his leg in a rather strange way. He had just ordered hot rum for the three of them.

"It's lonely country around here, gentlemen," he said.

"Yes," said Joe, "just marshes down to the river."

"Do people ever spend the night on the marshes?"

"No," replied Joe, "except an escaped prisoner sometimes. Difficult to find, they are. Went out to look for one once, me, and Mr. Wopsle, and young Pip here. Didn't we, Pip?"

"Yes, Joe."

The stranger looked at me with his good eye.

"What's his name? Pip? Your son, is he?"

"The boy is the blacksmith's wife's brother," explained Mr. Wopsle in his official church clerk's voice.

When the drinks arrived, the stranger did something that he wanted nobody to see except me. He mixed his hot rum and water, not with a spoon, but *with a file*, which he put back in his pocket when he had finished. As soon as I saw the file, I knew it was the one I had stolen from Joe, and I knew that this man knew my convict. I stared at him in horror.

The men continued their conversation in a friendly way until Joe stood up to leave and took my hand.

"Wait a moment," said the stranger. "I'd like to give the boy something," and wrapping a coin in some old paper from his pocket, he handed it to me. "That's yours!" he told me, giving

Not with a spoon, but with a file.

me a look full of meaning.

"Thank you, sir," I said, still staring at him. Together Joe and I walked home, Joe with his mouth open all the way so that my sister would not notice the smell of rum on his breath.

But when we arrived home, we found the stranger had given me two pound notes as well as the coin. My sister thought it must have been a mistake, and she kept the pound notes in case he came back for them. But I knew they came from my convict and I felt that having criminal friends made me more common than ever.

The next time I went to Miss Havisham's, I was shown into a different room to wait. Several ladies and gentlemen, relations of hers, were there. They all turned and looked at me in disgust when I was the first to be called by Estella.

As Estella was leading me along the dark passages, she stopped suddenly and put her face close to mine.

"Look at me, boy! Am I pretty?"

"Yes, I think you're very pretty."

"Am I rude to you?"

"Not as much as last time."

She hit my face as hard as she could.

"Now, you coarse little boy, what do you think of me?"

"I won't tell you."

"Why don't you cry again, you fool?"

"Because I'll never cry for you again," I said, which was a very false promise because I was crying inside at the time and only *I* know how much I cried for her later.

On our way upstairs we met a gentleman coming down in the dark. He was a large, heavy man, with a very dark skin, sharp eyes, and a huge head, almost bald on the top. His hands smelled strongly of perfumed soap. I didn't know then how important he would be later on in my life.

"Who's this?" he asked Estella, stopping to look at me.

"A local boy. Miss Havisham sent for him," she replied.

"Well, in my experience most boys are bad," he said to me. "Behave yourself!" He bit the side of his large finger as he frowned at me and then continued downstairs.

This time Miss Havisham was in another room, which I had not seen before. All the furniture was covered in dust. In the candle-light I could see a long table, in the middle of which was a large yellow shape, with hundreds of insects feeding off it.

"This," said Miss Havisham, pointing to the table, "is where they will put me when I'm dead. I'll lie on the table, and my relations can come and look at me." She put a bony hand on my shoulder, but I didn't want her to touch me. I was afraid she would die there and then. "And that," she added, pointing to the yellow shape, "that was my wedding cake. Mine!" She looked all around the room angrily. "Come!" she said suddenly. "Help me walk around the room. And call Estella!"

I held her arm to support her as she walked. We were still going slowly and painfully around the room when Estella brought in the relations who had been waiting downstairs. They stood watching us at the door. I thought they blamed me for Miss Havisham's cold manner towards them.

"Dear Miss Havisham!" said one of the ladies lovingly. "How well you look!"

"I do not," replied Miss Havisham sharply. "I am yellow skin and bone."

"How *could* Miss Havisham look well, after all her suffering?" said a second lady quickly. "Impossible! What a silly idea!"

"And how are *you*?" Miss Havisham asked this lady. As we were close to her then, I would have stopped, but Miss Havisham insisted on walking past. It seemed rather rude.

"Not well at all," said this lady sadly. "I don't want to talk too much about my feelings, but—well—I often lie awake at night thinking of you, dear Miss Havisham!"

"Well, don't!" said Miss Havisham crossly as we hurried past the little group again.

"I'm afraid I can't stop myself. I often wish I were less sensitive and loving. But that's my character and I have to live with it!" And she started crying softly. "Look at Matthew now!" she added, through her tears. "Matthew never comes to see dear Miss Havisham. But I—"

When she heard Matthew's name, Miss Havisham stopped walking and stood looking at the speaker, who suddenly became silent.

"Matthew will come in the end," said Miss Havisham firmly, "when I die and am laid on that table. You will stand around and look at me, you here, you there, you next to her, and you two there. Now you know where to stand. And now go!"

The ladies and gentlemen went slowly out of the room, some protesting quietly that they had not seen enough of their dear relation. When they had all gone, Miss Havisham said to me,

"This is my birthday, Pip. I don't allow anyone to speak of it. My relations always come on this day once a year. This day, long before you were born, was my wedding day. Perhaps I shall die on this day too. And when they lay me in my wedding dress on that table, I'll have my revenge on him!"

In the heavy air of that dark, dusty room, she was a ghostly figure in her yellow-white dress. There was a long silence.

As usual I left the house and walked towards the gate, but this time something strange happened. In the garden I met a pale young gentleman with fair hair.

"Hello!" he said. "Come and fight! This way!"

I was so surprised that I followed him without a word.

"Wait a minute," he said, turning around quickly. "I must give you a reason for fighting. There it is!" Then he pulled my hair and pushed his head hard into my stomach. I was ready to fight him after this, but he danced about so much that I couldn't get close to him.

"Follow the laws of the game!" he said, eagerly preparing himself for our fight. He seemed to know so much about fighting that I was very surprised when I knocked him down with my first hit and then again with my second. He always got up immediately and seemed very glad to be fighting in the correct manner. I admired him greatly for his bravery and his cheerfulness. Finally he had to agree I had won, and we said goodbye.

When I reached the gate, I found Estella waiting for me. She seemed very pleased about something. I wondered if she had been watching our fight. Before I went out, she said,

"Here! you can kiss me if you like."

I kissed her cheek. It was true I wanted to kiss her very much, but I felt that kiss was almost like a coin thrown to a poor common boy and not worth anything.

I didn't see the pale young gentleman there again. I continued my visits to Miss Havisham for almost a year. She took great pleasure in watching my growing admiration for Estella and my unhappiness when Estella laughed at me.

"Go on, my love," she used to whisper in Estella's ear, "break men's hearts, and have no mercy! I want my revenge!"

Meanwhile my sister and that fool Pumblechook never stopped discussing Miss Havisham and her considerable wealth. They were sure I could expect a large present from her, either before or after her death. But one day Miss Havisham decided it was time to apprentice me to Joe and told me to bring him to her house. My sister was very angry because she was not invited as well.

Dear old Joe simply could not believe his eyes when he and I entered Miss Havisham's room the next day. The darkness, the candles, the dust, the ancient furniture, and the old lady in her bride's dress—it was almost too much for Joe's limited intelligence. That may be why he refused to speak to Miss Havisham directly, but spoke only to me during the conversation. I was ashamed of him, especially as I could see Estella laughing at me over Miss Havisham's shoulder.

"So," began Miss Havisham, "you, Joe Gargery, blacksmith, are ready to take Pip as an apprentice?"

"You know, Pip," replied Joe, "how we've both been looking forward to working together. Haven't we, Pip?"

"You don't expect any payment when he becomes your apprentice?" she continued.

"Now, Pip," said Joe, rather offended, "that question doesn't need an answer. Between you and me. Does it, Pip?"

Miss Havisham looked kindly at Joe. I think she understood more of his character than Estella did. She picked up a little bag from the table. "Pip has earned something here. There are twenty-five pounds in this bag. Give it to your master, Pip."

The strange situation seemed to have made Joe go mad. Even now, he insisted on speaking to me.

"This is very generous of you, Pip. Very generous. Now, old boy, we must try to do our duty to each other. Mustn't we, Pip?"

"Goodbye, Pip!" said Miss Havisham. "Take them out, Estella!"

"Shall I come again?" I asked.

"No, Gargery is your master now. Gargery! Remember, I'm giving you this money because he has been a good boy. Don't expect anything more!"

Somehow I managed to get Joe out of the house, and in the daylight he gradually became normal again. In fact I think his intelligence was improved by the interview because as we walked home, he invented a surprisingly clever plan.

"Well," cried my sister, as we arrived, "so you've finished visiting your fine ladies, have you? I'm surprised you bother to come home at all!"

"Miss Havisham asked me to send," said Joe, as if trying to remember the exact words, "her—best wishes, was it, Pip? to Mrs. J. Gargery . . ."

"Best wishes," I agreed.

"And apologized for not being well enough, what was it, Pip?"

"To have the pleasure," I said.

"To have the pleasure of a lady's company," he nodded, giving the impression of a man glad to pass on a message correctly.

"Well!" said my sister, pleased. "She could have sent that message earlier, but better late than never. And what did she give the boy?"

"Nothing," said Joe firmly, stopping Mrs. Joe from speaking by raising his hand. "What she gave, she gave to his sister, Mrs. J. Gargery. That's what she said. Didn't she, Pip?"

"And how much did she give?" asked my sister, laughing. She was actually *laughing*!

"What would you say to ten pounds?" asked Joe.

"Not bad," said my sister.

"It's more than that. What would you say to twenty pounds?"

"That's good!" said my sister.

"Well, here you are—it's twenty-five pounds!" said Joe delightedly, handing the bag to my sister.

5

Pip's Sister Is Attacked

In a single year everything had changed. Before I went to Miss Havisham's and met Estella, I had always wanted to be apprenticed to Joe, and I had always been happy at home in spite of my sister's scolding. Now I was ashamed of my home and my work. I was very miserable. Because of Joe, however, I stayed at the forge and did my best to work hard. I'm glad that I never told him how unhappy I was then. I tried to follow his example and become an honest, happy, hardworking man. But all the time I thought of Estella. My worst fear was that one day she would come to the forge and see me working as a common blacksmith, with black face and hands. She would certainly turn away in disgust.

In the evenings I studied as hard as I could, educating myself for Estella. Whatever I learned, I shared with Joe, not, I'm afraid, so that he would be more educated, but so that I would be less ashamed of him in front of Estella. One Sunday Joe and I went out on the marshes, as usual, to study together. I don't think he ever remembered anything from one week to the next, but he smoked his pipe comfortably, looking as intelligent as he could. I had a question I had been intending to ask him.

"Joe, do you think I should visit Miss Havisham again?"

"Well, Pip," said Joe, "will she think you expect her to give you something? She told me she wouldn't give you anything else."

"But, Joe, I've been apprenticed nearly a year now, and I've never thanked her!"

"That's true, Pip," said Joe slowly.

"Could you give me a half day's holiday tomorrow, Joe? I *would* like to visit Miss Est—Havisham."

"Her name isn't Estavisham as far as I know, Pip," said Joe very seriously.

"I know, Joe! *Please*, Joe!"

"All right, Pip, but if she isn't happy to see you, better not go again."

Joe had another blacksmith working for him at the forge. His name was Orlick, and he had no friends or family in the village. He was a big, strong, lazy man, who moved about in a strangely unhurried way, his shoulders bent and his eyes on the ground. For some reason he never liked me, even when I was a child, and when I became Joe's apprentice, he seemed to hate me. When he heard about my half-day holiday, he threw down his hammer angrily.

"Come now, master!" he said to Joe. "If young Pip's having a holiday, give me one too!"

"Well," nodded Joe after thinking for a moment, "I will."

Just then my sister, who had secretly been listening outside the forge, called to Joe through one of the windows, "You fool! You think you're a rich man, giving a holiday to a lazy man like that Orlick! I wish *I* were his master! I'd soon show him!"

"You want to be everybody's master!" Orlick told her angrily. "And what's more, you're a wicked, ugly, old woman!"

"What did you say?" cried my sister, beginning to scream. "Oh! Oh! What did you call me? Hold me, someone!" Little by little she was deliberately making herself angry. Joe and I had seen this happen many times before.

"Hold you!" said Orlick in disgust. "If you were *my* wife, I'd hold you tight around the neck until you couldn't breathe!"

"Oh!" screamed my sister. "Me, a married woman! Being spoken to like this! In my own house! And my husband standing nearby! Oh! Oh!" And like a mad woman she pulled her hair loose and rushed at the forge door, which I had, luckily, locked.

Poor Joe had no choice. He had to challenge Orlick to fight. But Joe was the strongest man in the village, and very soon Orlick, like the pale young gentleman, was lying on the ground. Then Joe unlocked the door and picked up my sister, who had dropped unconscious to the ground, but only *after* watching the fight through the window. She stayed in the kitchen for the rest of the day, and Joe and Orlick shared a glass of beer peacefully together in the forge.

That afternoon when I arrived at Miss Havisham's house, it wasn't Estella who opened the gate, but a cousin of the old lady's. Miss Havisham looked just the same as before.

Very soon Orlick was lying on the ground.

"Well?" she said, "I hope you don't expect me to give you anything."

"No, indeed, Miss Havisham. I only want you to know that I'm very grateful to you for helping me become Joe's apprentice."

"Good. Come and see me again, on your birthday. Ah!" she cried suddenly, "you're looking for Estella, aren't you? Answer!"

"Ye—yes," I admitted. "I hope Miss Estella is well?"

"She's abroad, receiving a lady's education. She's more beautiful than ever and admired by all who see her. Do you feel you've lost her?" She gave such an unpleasant laugh with these last words that I didn't know what to say, and as I left the house, I felt even more miserable.

On my way through town I met Mr. Wopsle, and together we started the long walk home to the village. It was a dark, wet, misty night, and we could only just see someone ahead of us.

"Hello!" we called. "Is that Orlick?"

"Yes!" he answered. "I'll walk home with you. Been in town all afternoon, I have. Did you hear the big gun firing from the prison ships? Must be some prisoners who've escaped." That made me think of my convict. We didn't talk any more, but walked along in silence. We heard the gun firing several times.

It was late by the time we got to the village, and we were surprised to see lights on at the pub and people running in and out. Mr. Wopsle went in to discover what was happening, and after a few minutes he rushed out, calling, "Something wrong up at the forge, Pip! Run! They say perhaps it was an escaped convict who got into the house while Joe was out. Someone's been attacked!"

We didn't stop running until we reached the forge. In Mrs. Joe's kitchen there was a doctor, a group of women, and Joe. And on the floor in the middle of them all was my sister, lying unconscious. She would never scold us again.

Joe had been at the pub that evening, and when he arrived home just before ten, he found her on the floor. Nothing had been stolen. She had been hit violently on the back of the head with a heavy weapon. On the floor beside her was a convict's iron chain. It did not belong to the prisoners who had escaped that day.

The police spent the next week investigating the attack, but did not arrest anybody. I felt sure the iron chain belonged to my convict, but I did not think he had attacked my sister. The attacker could have been either Orlick or the stranger who had shown me the file. But several witnesses had seen Orlick in town all evening. My only reason for suspecting him was his quarrel with my sister, but she had quarreled with everyone in the village ten thousand times. And if the stranger had come to ask for his two pounds back, my sister would gladly have given it to him. So I could not imagine who her attacker was.

She lay ill in bed for a long time. She could not speak or understand much, and her character was greatly changed. She had become quiet, patient, and grateful for all our care. She used to write a word or draw a picture when she wanted something, and we tried to discover what she meant. She needed someone to take care of her all the time, and luckily old Mrs. Wopsle had just died, so Biddy came to live with us. She understood my sister perfectly and looked after us all very well.

One day my sister drew a T and seemed to want it very much. I brought her toast and tea, but Biddy knew immediately.

"It's not a T, it's Orlick's hammer!" she cried. "She's forgotten his name, but she wants to see Orlick!"

I must say I expected to see my sister accuse Orlick of attacking her, but instead she seemed very pleased to see him. She often used to ask for him after that, and nobody knew why.

One Sunday I asked Biddy to come for a walk on the marshes.

"Biddy," I said seriously, "promise to keep this a secret. I'm going to tell you something. I want to be a gentleman."

"Don't you think you're happier as you are?" she replied.

I had often wondered this myself, but I didn't want to hear it from her. "It's a pity, I know," I said. "It would have been much better if I could have been happy working at the forge. Perhaps you and I would have spent more time together. I would have been good enough for *you*, wouldn't I, Biddy?"

"Oh yes," she said sadly. "But I don't ask for very much."

"The point is," I continued crossly, "if nobody had told me I was coarse and common, I wouldn't have thought about it!"

Biddy looked at me, interested. "That wasn't a true or polite thing to say. Who said it?"

"It was the beautiful young lady at Miss Havisham's, and

I admire her greatly. I want to be a gentleman for her!" The words rushed out before I could stop them.

Biddy said gently, "She may not be worth the trouble, Pip."

"That may be true, but I can't stop myself admiring her."

Biddy was the most sensible of girls and did not try to persuade me any more. As we walked home, I felt rested and comforted.

"Pip, what a fool you are!" I said to myself. I realized how much happier I would always be with Biddy than with Estella.

"Biddy, I wish I could make myself fall in love with you!" I said suddenly. "You don't mind my speaking so openly, as you're such an old friend?"

"No, of course not. But you never will fall in love with me, you see," she answered, a little sadly.

I wondered if I should continue working with Joe in a plain, honest way of life and perhaps marry Biddy. Or dare I hope that Miss Havisham would make my fortune and marry me to Estella?

6

Great Expectations

One Saturday evening, when I had been apprenticed to Joe for four years, he and I were sitting in the pub with some of the villagers, listening to Mr. Wopsle. He was giving a dramatic reading of a newspaper report of a murder trial, and we all enjoyed watching him act the main characters. His witnesses were old and feeble, his lawyers were clever and sharp-eyed, and his accused was a violent, wicked murderer.

Suddenly we became aware of a strange gentleman who had also been listening and was now looking coldly at us.

"Well!" he said to us, biting the side of his finger. "So you've decided the accused was the murderer, have you?"

"Sir," answered Mr. Wopsle firmly, "yes, I do think he is guilty." We all nodded our heads in agreement.

"But," said the stranger, "do you or do you not know that the law of England supposes every man to be innocent until he is proved—*proved*—to be guilty?"

"Sir," began Mr. Wopsle, "as an Englishman myself, I—"

"Come!" said the stranger, "don't avoid the question. Either you know it, or you don't know it. Which is it?"

"Of course I know it," answered poor Mr. Wopsle.

"Then why didn't you say so at first? Another question. Do you know that this trial isn't finished yet?"

Mr. Wopsle hesitated, and we all began to have a rather bad opinion of him.

"And you were going to say that the accused was guilty *before* the end of the trial, *before* he has been proved guilty!" We realized that the unfortunate Wopsle had no understanding of the law, or indeed of anything at all.

Now the stranger stood in front of our little group.

"I'm looking for the blacksmith, Joe Gargery," he said, "and his apprentice, Pip." He did not recognize me, but I knew he was the gentleman I had met on the stairs when visiting Miss Havisham. There was even the same smell of perfumed soap on his large hands. "I want to speak to you two in private," he said, and so Joe and I left the pub and walked home with him.

"My name is Jaggers, and I'm a lawyer," he said, when he reached the forge. "Joe Gargery, I am sent by someone who suggests cancelling this boy's apprenticeship to you. Would you want any money if you lost your apprentice?"

"I'd never stand in Pip's way, never," said Joe, staring. "The answer is no."

"Don't try to change that answer later," said Mr. Jaggers. "Now, what I have to say, and remember—I'm only an agent, and I don't speak for myself—is that this young man has *great expectations*."

Joe and I gasped and looked at each other.

"I have been told to say that he will be very rich when he is older. In addition, the person who sent me wants the young man to be removed from his home and educated as a gentleman who expects to inherit a fortune."

My dream had come true. Miss Havisham was making me rich!

"Now, Mr. Pip," continued the lawyer, "there are two conditions. The first is that you always use the name of Pip. The

This young man has great expectations.

second is that the name of the person who has been so generous to you must remain a secret until that person chooses to tell you. You are forbidden to ask any questions or try to discover who the person is. Do you accept these conditions?"

My heart was beating fast as I whispered, "Yes."

"Now, to details. I have been given enough money for you to live the life of a gentleman in London while you are studying. You will come to me to ask for whatever you need. I suggest Mr. Matthew Pocket as a teacher." I remembered that was the name of one of Miss Havisham's relations, the one who did not visit her often. "You must buy some new clothes. Shall I leave you twenty pounds?" He counted twenty coins out of his large purse on to the table. "And when can you come to London? Next Saturday?"

I agreed, feeling very confused. He looked at Joe, who seemed even more confused.

"Well, Joe Gargery? Perhaps, I only say perhaps—I promise nothing," he said, throwing his purse carelessly from one hand to another, "*perhaps* I have been told to give you a present when you lose your apprentice."

Joe put his great strong hand on my shoulder in the gentlest possible way. "Pip can go freely to fortune and happiness—he knows that. But if you think that *money* can ever pay me back for losing the little child—who came to the forge—and always the best of friends! . . ." He could not continue.

Dear good Joe! I was so ready to leave you and so ungrateful to you! I can see you now, with your strong blacksmith's arm in front of your eyes, your shoulders shaking, and tears on your cheeks. But at the time I was so excited by my good luck that I forgot what I owed to Joe. Mr. Jaggers clearly thought Joe was a fool for refusing money and left the house, reminding me to go straight to his office in London in a week's time.

Joe told Biddy what had happened and both congratulated me. They were very quiet and sad at first because I would be leaving them, but I promised I would never forget them and would often return to visit them. Biddy tried to explain the good news to my sister, but the poor woman could not understand.

As Joe and Biddy became a little more cheerful, discussing my possible plans for the future, I became more miserable. Now that I could be a gentleman as I had always wished, I was not sure if I wanted to leave my home, which was full of happy memories.

That week passed slowly. I took a last walk through the churchyard to the marshes. At least I need never think about my convict again. No doubt he was dead by now.

I had something special to ask Biddy. "Biddy," I said, when we were alone, "don't you think you could teach Joe a bit?"

"What do you mean, teach him?" asked Biddy.

"Well, I love dear old Joe more than anyone else, but his education and manners could be improved."

Biddy opened her eyes very wide. "Oh?" she said. "So his manners aren't good enough, then?"

"Oh, they're all right for *here*, but when I receive my fortune, I'll want him to meet important people and behave correctly."

"Haven't you ever thought," asked Biddy, not looking at me, "that he wouldn't *want* to meet important people, he wouldn't *want* to be taken away from this job that he does well and the village where he's loved?"

"Now, Biddy," I said crossly, "are you jealous of my good luck? I didn't expect this of you. This is a bad side of your character, Biddy."

"Whether you scold me or thank me, I'll always do my best for the family at all times. And I'll always remember you, whatever you think of me," said poor Biddy.

I was not pleased with this interview, and I thought it was strange that the news of my expectations had not made me happier.

When I went into town to order my new clothes, Mr. Pumblechook was waiting for me at the door of his shop.

"My dear friend, if you will allow me to call you that," he cried, shaking both my hands, "let me congratulate you on your fortune! Nobody deserves it more than you!" He seemed so much more sensible than before that I agreed to have lunch with him.

"When I think," he said happily, "that *I*, Pumblechook, was able to help in my small way, by taking you to play at Miss—"

"Remember," I stopped him, "we must never say anything about the person who is being so generous to me."

"Don't worry, trust me, my dear friend. Have some wine, have some chicken! Oh chicken, you didn't think when you were running around on the farm that you would be lucky enough to be served to one who—May I? *May* I?" and he jumped up to shake my hand again.

As we drank our wine, Pumblechook reminded me of the happy times he and I had spent together during my childhood. I did not remember it quite like that, but I began to feel he was a good-hearted, sincere man. He wanted to ask my advice on a business matter. He said he was hoping to find a young gentleman who would put money into his business, and he seemed very interested in my opinion. "And may I? *May* I?" He shook hands with me again.

"You know, I always used to say, 'That boy will make his fortune. He's no ordinary boy.'" He had certainly kept his opinion very secret, I thought.

There was one person I really wanted to visit before going

to London. Dressed in my new clothes I went to Miss Havisham's house, where her cousin opened the gate to me again.

"Well, Pip?" said Miss Havisham to me when she saw me.

"I'm going to London tomorrow, Miss Havisham," I said, choosing my words carefully, "and I wanted to say goodbye. I've been so lucky since I saw you last, and I'm so grateful for it!"

"Good, good!" she replied, looking delightedly at her cousin who was staring at my new clothes. "I know about it. I've seen Mr. Jaggers. So, a rich person has adopted you?"

"Yes, Miss Havisham."

She smiled cruelly at her cousin, who was looking rather ill.

"Remember to do what Mr. Jaggers tells you. And you will always keep the name of Pip, won't you? Goodbye, Pip." She gave me her hand, and I kissed it. It seemed the natural thing to do. And so I left the old lady in her bride's dress in the candle-light, with the dusty furniture around her.

On Saturday morning I was in such a hurry that I only said a quick goodbye to my family before setting out to walk the few miles into town for the London coach. As I left the peaceful sleeping village, the mist over the marshes was rising to show me the great unknown world I was entering. Suddenly I realized what I was leaving behind—my childhood, my home, and Joe. Then I wished I had asked him to walk with me to the coach, and I could not stop crying. Whenever the horses were changed on the journey, I wondered with an aching heart whether to get down and go back to say goodbye properly. But the mist had completely risen now, and my new world lay ahead of me.

7

Pip Arrives in London

At that time everybody in England agreed that London was a wonderful city. So I was surprised to find it rather ugly, with narrow dirty streets and people crowded into tiny houses. I was frightened by its huge size. At Smithfield, the meat market, I was shocked by the dirt and blood everywhere. Then I came to Newgate Prison, where a drunk old man showed me the place where prisoners were hanged and told me excitedly that four men would die there tomorrow. I was disgusted by this news. My first impression of London could not have been worse.

However, I managed to find Mr. Jaggers' office, noticing that other people were waiting for the great man too. After some time he appeared, walking towards me. His clients all rushed at him together. He spoke to some and pushed others away. One man held on to the lawyer's sleeve.

"Please, Mr. Jaggers," he begged, "my brother is accused of stealing silver. Only you can save him! I'm ready to pay anything!"

"Your brother?" repeated the lawyer. "And the trial is tomorrow? Well, I'm sorry for you, and for him as well. I'm on the other side."

"No, Mr. Jaggers!" cried the man desperately, tears in his eyes. "Don't say you're against him! I'll pay anything!"

"Get out of my way," said Mr. Jaggers, and we left the man on his knees on the pavement.

Now Mr. Jaggers turned to me and told me that on Monday I would go to Matthew Pocket's house to start my studies, but until then I would stay with his son, Herbert, who lived nearby.

Wemmick, Mr. Jaggers' clerk, showed me the way to Mr. Pocket's rooms. He was a short, dry man, with a square, expressionless face, between forty and fifty years old. His mouth was so wide that it looked like a post-box and gave the impression of smiling all the time.

"Is London a very wicked place?" I asked him, trying to make conversation as we walked.

"You may be robbed or murdered in London. But that may happen to you anywhere if there is any profit in it for the criminal."

I was not sure whether I looked forward to living in London,

His clients all rushed at him together.

where people like Wemmick accepted crime so calmly.

We arrived at Herbert Pocket's rented rooms. The building was the dirtiest I had ever seen, with broken windows and dusty doors. It stood in a little square with dying trees around it. I looked in horror at Mr. Wemmick.

"Ah!" he said, not understanding my look. "Its quiet position makes you think of the country. I quite agree. Goodbye, Mr. Pip."

I went up the stairs, where there was a note on Mr. Pocket's door, saying "Returning soon." His idea of "soon" was not the same as mine. About half an hour later I heard footsteps rushing upstairs, and a young man of my age appeared breathless at the door. "Mr. Pip?" he said. "I'm so sorry I'm late!"

I greeted him in a confused manner, unable to believe my eyes. Suddenly he looked closely at me and gasped.

"But you're the boy at Miss Havisham's!"

"And you," I said, "are the pale young gentleman!"

We both started laughing and shook hands.

"Well!" he said, "I hope you'll forgive me for having knocked you down that day." In fact *I* had knocked *him* down. But I did not contradict him.

"Do you know why I was there?" he asked. "I had been invited to Miss Havisham's to see if she liked me. I suppose I didn't make a good impression on her. If she had liked me, I could be a rich man and engaged to Estella by now."

"Were you disappointed?" I asked.

"Oh! I wouldn't want to marry Estella! She's a hard, proud girl, and Miss Havisham has brought her up to break men's hearts, as a revenge on all men."

"Is she a relation of Miss Havisham's?" I asked.

"No, only adopted. Why were *you* at Miss Havisham's then?"

"To make my fortune, the same as you! But I was lucky."

"You know Mr. Jaggers is Miss Havisham's lawyer? It was kind of him to suggest that my father should teach you. My father is Miss Havisham's cousin, you know."

Herbert Pocket made an excellent impression on me. He always spoke openly and honestly. There was nothing secret or mean in his character, and we soon became good friends. I told him of my past life in the village and my expectations.

"Call me Herbert," he said. "Would you mind my calling you Handel? There's a wonderful piece of music by Handel, called The Blacksmith, which reminds me of you." Of course I agreed, and as we sat down to dinner, Herbert told me Miss Havisham's sad story.

"Her mother died young. Her father was very rich and very proud, with only one child, Miss Havisham, by his first wife. Then he married his cook and had a son by her. This son, a half-brother to Miss Havisham, was a bad character and didn't inherit as much from his father as Miss Havisham did. And so perhaps he was angry with her for influencing her father against him.

"Anyway, a certain man appeared and pretended he was in love with Miss Havisham. She was certainly in love with him, and she gave him whatever money he asked for. My father was the only one of her relations who dared to tell her that this man should not be trusted. She was so angry that she ordered my father straight out of the house, and he has never seen her since. Her other relations were not interested in her happiness but only in inheriting her wealth, so they said nothing. The couple fixed the wedding day, the guests were invited, and the dress and the cake were brought to the house. The day came, but the man did not. He wrote a letter—"

"Which she received at twenty to nine, when she was dressing for her wedding?" I said.

"Yes, so she stopped the clocks at that moment. She was very ill for a while, and since then she has not seen daylight. People think that her half-brother sent the man to get money from her and that he shared the profits. Perhaps he hated her for inheriting most of the Havisham fortune. Nobody knows what happened to the two men. So now you know as much as I do!"

We talked of other things. I asked Herbert what his profession was.

"Oh, working in the City," he said happily. "Insuring ships. There's a lot of money in that, you know. Huge profits!"

I began to think that Herbert must have greater expectations than I had.

"Where are your ships at the moment?" I asked admiringly.

"Oh, I haven't started yet. I'm working in a counting-house just now. They don't pay me much, but I'm looking about me for a good opportunity. *Then* I'll make my fortune!"

Looking around the room, at the old, worn furniture, I realized that Herbert must be very poor. And although he seemed full of hope for the future, somehow I thought he would never be very rich or successful.

He and I spent a happy weekend visiting London together. Although it was all very exciting, I could not avoid noticing the dirt, bad smells, and heat, and I compared it sadly with my village home, which now seemed so far away.

8

Visiting Mr. Wemmick and Mr. Jaggers

Herbert introduced me to his father, who lived on the other side of London, in Hammersmith. In the next few months I studied hard with Mr. Pocket, who was always a most kind and helpful teacher. I divided my time between Herbert's and his father's home. If I needed money, I collected it from Wemmick at Mr. Jaggers' office, and there seemed to be plenty of money available.

There were two other gentlemen studying at Mr. Pocket's. They were quite different from each other. Bentley Drummle came from a rich family living in the country. He was lazy, proud, mean, and stupid. I much preferred Startop, who was a pleasant, sensitive young man. He and I used to row our boats up and down the river together. But Herbert was my greatest friend, and we used to spend most of our time with each other.

One day when I was collecting my money from Wemmick, he invited me to his house at Walworth, a village outside London.

"You don't mind walking there, Mr. Pip?" he asked. "I like to get some exercise if I can. For dinner we're having a roast chicken. I think it'll be a good one because I got it from one of our clients. I always accept any little presents from clients, especially if it's cash, or anything that can easily be changed into cash. You see these rings I'm wearing? Given by clients, just before they died. All hanged, they were. By the way, I hope you won't mind meeting my aged parent?"

"No, of course not," I said quickly.

"You haven't had dinner with Mr. Jaggers yet?" Wemmick continued. "He's inviting you and the other three young gentlemen tomorrow. There'll be good food and drink at his house. But I'll tell you something, Mr. Pip. When you're there, look at his housekeeper."

"Why?" I asked. "Is there something strange about her?"

"She's like a wild animal. But Mr. Jaggers has trained her! Oh yes! He's stronger, cleverer, and more complicated than anyone else in London. And you know, another strange thing about him—he never locks his doors or windows at night."

"Isn't he ever robbed?" I asked in surprise.

"All the thieves in London know where he lives, but none of them would dare to rob him. They are all afraid of him, you see. They know he wouldn't rest until he had seen them hanged. He's a great man, Mr. Pip."

Wemmick's house at Walworth was a tiny wooden house in the middle of a garden. On top of the roof was a small gun.

"We fire the gun at nine o'clock every evening," said Wemmick proudly. "And behind the house—I call it the Castle—I keep animals and grow my own vegetables. So, in case of enemy attack, we can always eat our own food. What do you think of it?"

I congratulated him on his home. He was clearly delighted to show a visitor all his ideas and improvements.

"I do everything myself, you know," he said. "It helps me forget the office for a while. Would you mind being introduced to the Aged now? He would like it very much."

So we entered the Castle, where we found a cheerful old man sitting by the fire.

"Well, aged parent," said Wemmick, "how are you?"

"Very well, John," replied the old man, nodding happily.

"Here's Mr. Pip, aged parent. Nod your head at him, Mr. Pip, he's completely deaf, but he likes to see people nod at him."

"This is a fine house of my son's, sir," cried the old man,

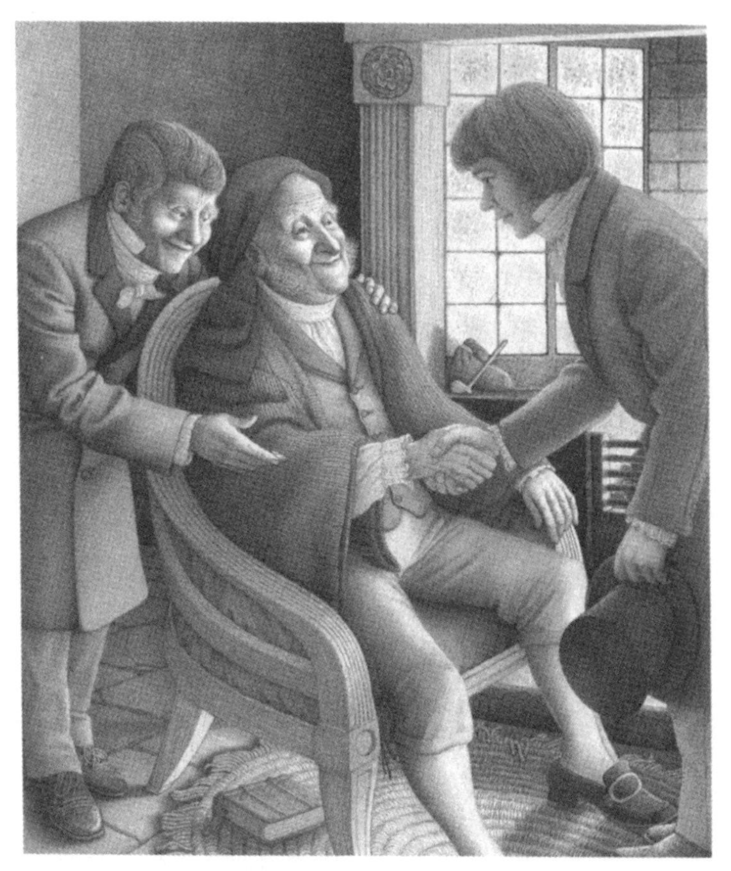

"Here's Mr. Pip, aged parent."

nodding back at me. "It should be kept by the nation for the public to visit after my son's death."

"You're proud of it, aren't you, Aged?" said Wemmick, his face losing all its usual hardness as he looked at the old man.

"I hope Mr. Jaggers admires your home, Mr. Wemmick?" I asked.

"He's never been here. Never met the Aged. Never been invited. No, the office is one thing, and private life is another.

At the office I never speak of the Castle, and at the Castle I don't think about the office."

The Aged was obviously looking forward to the evening ceremony of firing the gun. At nine o'clock exactly Wemmick fired it. As the tiny house shook, the Aged jumped up and down in his armchair, crying excitedly, "I heard it! That's the gun!"

Supper was excellent, and I spent the night in the smallest bedroom I had ever seen. Next morning, as Wemmick and I walked back to London, I noticed his face becoming dryer and harder and his mouth becoming more like a post-box again. When we arrived at the office, nobody could have guessed that he had a home, or an aged parent, or any interests at all outside his work.

Wemmick was right in saying that Mr. Jaggers would invite me to dinner. Startop, Drummle, Herbert, and I were asked to go to the office at six o'clock the next evening. There we found Jaggers washing his hands and face carefully with perfumed soap. He did this every evening before going home. He seemed to be washing away his clients and his work, like dirt. We all walked to his house together.

The housekeeper brought in the first dish. She was about forty, with a strange wild expression on her pale face. She seemed almost afraid of her master and looked anxiously at him whenever she entered the room.

The food was indeed very good, and the conversation was cheerful. But somehow Mr. Jaggers made us all show the worst side of our characters and encouraged Drummle, who we all disliked, to annoy us. When Drummle stupidly said that he was stronger than any of us, we all protested, foolishly showing each other our muscles to prove how strong we were. Suddenly Mr. Jaggers clapped his large hand on the housekeeper's, as she was removing a dish. We stopped talking immediately.

"Gentlemen," he said, "look at my housekeeper here. She

is stronger than any of you. Molly, show them your wrists."

"No, please, master," she begged, trying to pull away, but he held her hand firmly.

"Show them, Molly," he said, and she held her wrists out to us. "I've never seen stronger hands than these," he said. There was silence for a few minutes. "All right, Molly, you can go," he said, and she hurried out.

During the rest of the dinner, Mr. Jaggers continued to enjoy watching us quarreling with Drummle. He gave the impression, surprisingly, of liking Drummle very much. But I was glad when the dinner was over, and Herbert and I could walk quietly back to our rooms together.

9

A Visit from Joe

"My dear Pip,

Mr. Gargery asks me to tell you he will be in London soon and could visit you at 9 o'clock on Tuesday morning at Mr. Herbert Pocket's rooms if that is all right with you. He and I talk about you every night and wonder what you are saying and doing.

Best wishes,

Biddy.

P.S. I hope you will not refuse to see him even though you are a gentleman now. He is such a good man."

I received this letter on Monday and realized that Joe would arrive the next day. I am sorry to confess that I did not look forward to seeing him at all. If I could have kept him away by paying money, I certainly would have paid money. I knew that his clothes, his manners, and uneducated way of speaking would make me ashamed of him. Luckily Herbert would not laugh at him.

At nine o'clock the next morning I heard Joe's clumsy boots on the stairs, and at last he entered Herbert's rooms.

"Pip, how *are* you, Pip?" He shook both my hands together, his good honest face shining with happiness.

"I'm glad to see you, Joe. Give me your hat."

But Joe insisted on holding it carefully in front of him. He was wearing his best suit, which did not fit him at all.

"Well! What a gentleman you are now, Pip!"

"And you look wonderfully well, Joe."

"Yes, thank God. And your poor sister is no worse. And Biddy is as hard-working as ever. But Wopsle isn't our church clerk any longer! He's become an actor! Acting in one of your London theaters, he is!" Joe's eyes rolled around the room, noticing the expensive furniture I had bought recently.

"Do sit down to breakfast, Mr. Gargery," said Herbert politely. Joe looked around desperately for a place to put his hat and finally laid it lovingly on a shelf. Breakfast was a painful experience for me. Joe waved his fork in the air so much and dropped so much more than he ate that I was glad when Herbert left to go to work. I was not sensitive enough to realize that it was all my fault, and that if I hadn't considered him common he wouldn't have been so clumsy.

"As we are now alone, sir—" began Joe.

"Joe," I said crossly, "how can you call me sir?"

He looked at me quietly for a moment. "Wouldn't have come, you see," he said slowly and carefully. "Wouldn't have had the pleasure of breakfast with you gentlemen. But I *had* to come. Got a message for you, Pip. Miss Havisham says Estella's

Breakfast was a painful experience for me.

come home and would be glad to see you."

I felt the blood rush to my face as I heard her name.

"And now I've given my message," said Joe, standing up and picking up his hat. "Pip, I wish you even more success."

"But you aren't leaving already, Joe?" I protested.

"Yes, I am," he said firmly. Our eyes met, and all the "sir" melted out of his honest heart as he gave me his hand. "Pip, dear old boy, life is full of so many goodbyes. I'm a blacksmith, and you're a gentleman. We must live apart. I'm not proud—it's just that I want to be in the right place. I'm wrong in these clothes, and I'm wrong in London, but I'm fine at the forge, or in the kitchen, or on the marshes. You won't find so much wrong with me if you come to see Joe, the blacksmith, at the old forge, doing the old work. I know I'm stupid, but I think I've understood this at last. And so God *bless* you, Pip, dear old boy, God bless you!"

His words, spoken simply and from the heart, touched me deeply. By the time I had managed to control my tears and looked around for him, he had gone.

I decided to visit Miss Havisham as soon as possible. Next day, when I arrived to take my seat on the coach to our town, I discovered I was sitting in front of two convicts, who were being taken to the prison ships by their guard. The prisoners wore handcuffs and iron chains on their legs. With horror I suddenly recognized one of them—it was the man in our village pub who had given me the two pound notes—and strangely enough, during the journey I heard the prisoners talking about it!

"So Magwitch asked you to give the boy two pounds? Trusted you to do it?"

"That's right. And I did what he asked. The boy had helped him, you see. Fed him and kept his secret."

"What happened to Magwitch in the end?"

"They sent him to Australia for life because he tried to escape from the prison ship."

I knew I looked so different that he would not recognize me, but I was afraid all the same. All the horror of my childhood experience with the escaped convict had come back to me, just when I thought it was safe to forget it.

But once we had arrived and I was on my way to Miss Havisham's house, I thought only of my bright future. She had adopted Estella; she had more or less adopted me. She perhaps wanted me to inherit the dark old house and to marry Estella. But even though I was in love, I didn't hide from myself the fact that I would be unhappy with Estella. I loved her because I couldn't stop myself loving her.

I was surprised to see Orlick opening the gate to me.

"So you aren't working for Joe any longer?" I asked.

"As you see, young master," he said rudely.

I knew he could not be trusted, and I decided to tell Mr. Jaggers that Orlick was not responsible enough to work for Miss Havisham. Mr. Jaggers would probably send him away.

When I entered Miss Havisham's room, there was a well-dressed lady sitting with her. When she lifted her head and looked at me, I realized it was Estella. She had become so beautiful that I felt very distant from her. In spite of all my education, I still seemed to be the coarse, common boy she used to laugh at.

"She's changed very much, hasn't she, Pip?" asked Miss Havisham, laughing wickedly. I replied confusedly. I could see that Estella was still proud, and I knew that it was she who made me feel ashamed of home and Joe, but I also knew that I could never stop loving her.

She and I walked in the ancient garden, talking quietly about our childhood meetings. Now that we were adults, she seemed to accept me as a friend. I could not have been happier. I felt sure Miss Havisham had chosen us for each other. What a fool I was!

Suddenly she stopped and turned to me. "Miss Havisham may want us to spend more time together in future. But in that case I must warn you that I have no heart. I can never fall in love."

"I can't believe that," I replied. As she looked straight at me,

I recognized something in her face. Had I seen that expression recently, on another woman?

When we went back to the house, Miss Havisham spoke to me alone. "Do you admire her, Pip?" she asked eagerly.

"Everybody who sees her must admire her."

She pulled my head down to hers with her bony arm and whispered, "Love her, love her, love her! If she likes you, love her! If she hurts you, love her! If she tears your heart to pieces, love her!" I could feel the muscles on her thin arm around my neck. She seemed so angry that she could have been talking about hate, or revenge, or death, rather than love.

10

Pip and Herbert Talk about Love

I returned to London, dreaming of the beautiful girl, now a woman, who had so influenced my childhood, and who, I hoped, would share my future life. I am sorry to say I did not think about dear, good Joe at all. I felt I had to express my feelings to someone, and so that evening I told Herbert my secret.

Instead of being surprised, as I expected, my friend replied, "I know that already, Handel. You never told me, but it was obvious. You've always loved Estella. It's very lucky that you seem to have been chosen to marry her. Does she, er, admire you?"

I shook my head sadly. "Not at all. And Herbert, you may think me lucky. I have great expectations, I know. But all that depends on one person! And I still don't really know how much I'll receive, or when! Nothing is certain!"

"Now, Handel," said Herbert cheerfully, "don't lose hope. Mr. Jaggers himself told you you would have a large fortune, didn't he? He would never make a mistake about something like that. Anyway, you'll be twenty-one soon. Perhaps you'll discover more then."

"Thank you, Herbert!" I said, feeling much better.

"But I want to ask you something, my dear Handel," said Herbert, looking serious for once. "Think of Estella, and her education, and how unhappy you may be with her. Couldn't you possibly—and I'm saying this as a friend, remember—couldn't you forget about her?"

"I know you're right, Herbert," I said miserably, "but I can never stop loving her."

"Well, never mind!" said Herbert. "Now I have something to tell you myself. I am engaged."

"May I ask the young lady's name?"

"Clara. Her mother's dead, and she lives with her father. We must keep our feelings for each other secret, because I don't have enough money to marry her yet. As soon as I start insuring ships, we can marry." Herbert tried to look hopeful about his future, but this time he couldn't even manage his usual cheerful smile.

One day I received a letter which made my heart beat fast.

"I am coming to London the day after tomorrow by the mid-day coach. Miss Havisham wants you to meet me.

Estella."

If there had been time, I would have ordered several new suits. I ate nothing until the day arrived, and all morning I waited impatiently for the coach. She seemed more beautiful than ever, and her manner to me was very pleasant as I took her to the house in London where Miss Havisham had arranged for her to stay. Her life seemed to be planned by Miss Havisham right down to the smallest detail. I only hoped I was part of that plan.

11

Pip Attends a Burial

One evening a black-edged envelope was delivered to me at Herbert's rooms. The letter inside informed me that Mrs. J. Gargery had died the previous Monday and that the burial would be next Monday, at 3 p.m. This news came as a shock to me. It was the first time that someone close to me had died, and I could not imagine life without my sister, even if I had never loved her or even thought about her recently.

I arrived at the forge early on Monday afternoon. Joe was sitting in the front room, wrapped in a black cloak.

"Dear Joe, how are you?" I asked.

"Pip, dear old boy, you knew her when she was a fine woman . . ." and he could say no more.

Biddy, in her neat little black dress, was busy serving food. Old friends from the village were talking quietly among themselves, and I noticed the awful Pumblechook trying to catch my eye, as he drank brandy and swallowed large pieces of cake.

"May I, my dear sir? *May* I?" he asked, his mouth full, and he shook my hand enthusiastically.

My sister's dead body was carried slowly out of the house and through the village, followed by all of us. We could see the marshes and the sails of ships on the river. And there, in the churchyard, next to my unknown parents, my poor sister was laid quietly in the earth, while the birds sang and the clouds danced in the sky.

Biddy, Joe, and I felt better when all the guests had gone, and we had a quiet supper together. I decided to spend the night at the forge, which pleased Joe very much. I was pleased with myself for offering to do so.

I waited until I found Biddy alone. Then I said, "I suppose you won't be able to stay here now, will you, Biddy?"

"No, Mr. Pip. I'll stay in the village, but I'll still look after Mr. Gargery as much as I can."

"How are you going to live, Biddy? If you want any money—"

"I'm going to be the village schoolteacher," she said quickly, her cheeks pink. "I can earn my own money."

"Tell me, Biddy, how did my sister die?"

"She had been worse than usual when one evening she said, very clearly, 'Joe.' And so I ran to the forge to get him. And she put her arms around his neck and laid her head on his shoulder, quite happy. Once she said 'Sorry', and once 'Pip.' She never lifted her head up again, and an hour later she died."

Biddy cried, and I cried too.

"What happened to Orlick, Biddy?"

"He's still in the village. He doesn't work for Miss Havisham any more. You know, he—he follows me sometimes."

"You must tell me if he bothers you, Biddy. I'll be here more often now. I'm not going to leave poor Joe alone."

Biddy said nothing.

"Come, Biddy, what do you mean by this silence?"

"Are you quite sure, then, that you *will* come to see him?"

"Oh Biddy!" I said sadly. "This really is a bad side to your character! Don't say any more!" And that evening I thought how unkind, how unjust Biddy was to me.

Next morning I looked in at the forge before leaving and said goodbye to Joe, who was already hard at work.

"I shall be back to see you soon, Joe!"

"Never too soon, sir," said Joe, "and never too often, Pip!"

As I walked away, I think I knew that I would not go back. Biddy was right.

In London, I did some serious thinking. I could see that my character had not improved since I had heard about my expectations. I was spending far too much money. What was worse, I was a bad influence on Herbert, who was also spending too much. I would have offered to pay his bills, but he was too proud to listen to such a suggestion. I had hoped that on my twenty-first birthday I would discover more about my future, but Mr. Jaggers explained that he could not give me any more information, except that from now on I would have five hundred pounds a year to spend as I liked. I suddenly thought of a way I could help Herbert.

When I asked Wemmick if he could advise me on how to help a friend start up in business, his post-box mouth opened wide.

"Choose one of the six London bridges," he said, "and throw your money over it. That's better than investing money for a friend. That's my official opinion, of course."

"Ah, so you would give me a different opinion at Walworth?"

"You'll be welcome there, Mr. Pip, on *private* business."

Next Sunday I visited Wemmick and his aged parent at the Castle. This time there was a lady called Miss Skiffins, clearly a regular visitor, who made the tea and sat next to Wemmick on the sofa. When he and I were alone, Wemmick listened carefully to my request and, after thinking hard, found an answer.

With his help I arranged to invest some money in a shipping company called Clarrikers. Finally I signed an agreement with them, in which they promised to offer Herbert a job and later to make him a partner. At last I felt that my expectations had done some good to someone.

12

Pip Discovers the Truth

While Estella lived in London, staying with friends of Miss Havisham's, I often visited her. She had an endless stream of admirers, and I was jealous of all of them. I never had an hour's happiness with her, but I still thought about her, day and night, and my dearest wish was to marry her. Several times Miss Havisham ordered me to bring Estella to visit her, and of course I always obeyed. Estella was as proud and cold as ever, with her admirers, with Miss Havisham, and with me.

One man who admired her and followed her everywhere was the unpleasant Bentley Drummle. One day I asked her about him.

"Estella, why do you encourage someone like Drummle? You know very well he's stupid and nobody likes him."

"Don't be foolish, Pip," she answered. "Perhaps I encourage him because that has a certain effect on the others."

"But he isn't worth it!" I cried angrily.

"What difference does it make?" she answered tiredly. "If I smile at him, it's because it means nothing to me. You should be glad that I don't give *you* false looks or smiles. At least I am always honest with *you*."

But while my heart was aching for Estella, I had no idea that I would soon be hit by a disaster which would completely destroy my hopes and dreams. The chain of events which had begun before I ever met her was slowly reaching its end.

Herbert and I had moved to rooms in a house by the river, in the Temple area. One evening he was abroad on business, and I was alone at home, reading. It was terrible weather, stormy and wet, with deep mud in the streets. The wind rushing up the river shook the whole building, and the rain beat violently against the windows. As I closed my book at eleven o'clock, I heard a heavy footstep on the stairs. When I went to the door with my lamp, I saw a man coming slowly upstairs. He was

I saw a man coming slowly upstairs.

wearing rough clothes, and he was about sixty, with a brown face and long gray hair. But what really surprised me was that he was holding out both hands to me.

"Can I help you?" I asked politely but coldly.

"Ah! Yes," he said, dropping his hands, "yes, I'll explain." He came into the sitting-room, where he looked around admiringly at my furniture and books. He held out his hands to me again, but I refused to take them. Then he sat down heavily in a chair and rubbed his eyes with one rather dirty hand.

"You see," he said, "it's disappointing. Looked forward to this day for so long, I have. But it's not your fault. I'll explain. Is there anybody near who can hear us?"

"Why do you, a stranger, visiting me late at night, ask that question?" I asked. And then suddenly I knew who he was! In spite of the years that had passed, I was sure he was my convict! And when he held out his hands again, this time I took them. He raised my hands to his lips and kissed them.

"You helped me all those years ago, Pip! Never forgotten it!" He seemed to want to put his arms around me, but I stopped him.

"If you are grateful to me for what I did in my childhood, I hope you have improved your way of life now. It wasn't necessary to come here to thank me. But you must understand that . . ." I stopped speaking as I noticed how strangely he was staring at me.

"What must I understand?" he asked, his eyes fixed on me.

"That I don't wish to be your friend. You and I met once in the past, but now our lives are separate. Will you have a drink before you leave?" As I handed him a glass of rum, I noticed that his eyes were full of tears. "I'm sorry if that sounds hard," I added. "I didn't mean it to be. Good luck in the future!" We drank together. "How have you been living recently?"

"I was sent to Australia, you know, because I escaped from the prison ship. After several years I finished my punishment, and so I was allowed to work for myself. I did every kind of job there. It was a hard life, but I made a lot of money."

"I'm glad to hear it," I said. "That reminds me, I must give you back the two pounds you sent me. I don't need it now." And I handed him two new pound notes from my purse. Still watching me, he held them near the lamp until they caught fire.

"May I ask," he said, "how *you* have done so well since you and I met on those lonely marshes?" His eyes were still fixed on mine, and I began to tremble.

"I—I've been chosen to inherit a fortune," I whispered.

"Perhaps I can guess how much," said the convict. "Could it be, well, five hundred pounds a year?" I stood up, holding on to the back of my chair, my heart beating like a hammer.

"The agent who arranged it all," he continued, "was he perhaps a lawyer, name of Jaggers?"

Suddenly I realized the awful truth. I could not speak nor breathe, and I fell on to the sofa. He brought his fierce old face close to mine and bent over me.

"Yes, Pip, dear boy, I've made a gentleman of you! You see, I promised myself that all the money I earned out there in Australia should go to you! I'm your second father, Pip! I'm not a gentleman myself, and I didn't go to school, but I've got *you*, Pip! And look what a gentleman you are! And what books you've got! You'll read them to me, Pip! And I'll be proud of you even if I can't understand them! Didn't you ever think it could be me who was sending the money?"

"Oh no, no, no," I replied. "Never, never! Wasn't anyone else involved at all?"

"No, just me, and Jaggers, of course. Who else could there be? Dear boy, I kept myself going, you see, through all the hard work, just by thinking of you. And I promised myself I'd come back to England one day and see my boy." He laid his hand on my shoulder. "Now you must find a bed for me," he added, "and remember, not a word to anybody. I was sent away for life, and they'll hang me if they discover I've come back."

My feelings were horribly confused. The man who had paid for my education and luxuries for years was risking his life to see me. I could not like him—in fact my whole body trembled with disgust when he touched me, but I had to protect him.

He went to sleep in Herbert's room. After locking all the doors carefully, I sat weakly down by the fire and tried to make sense of my life. How foolish my dreams had been! Miss Havisham had never intended to make me rich or let me marry Estella. But there was something worse than that. It was for this convict, who could be caught and hanged at any moment, that I had deserted Joe. I could never, never, never forgive myself for that.

13

Planning Magwitch's Future and Hearing about His Past

I slept a little, but woke early. I felt I needed some fresh air and went downstairs and out of the building. On the way down I fell over a man hiding in a dark corner, who ran away immediately. This worried me. I suspected he had followed my convict to the house. Would he now inform the police?

My guest and I had breakfast together. He ate noisily and greedily, like an animal. I tried hard not to be disgusted by his manners. He told me his name was Abel Magwitch, and after breakfast he lit his pipe and held out his hands for mine again.

"All I want is to stand and look at you, dear boy!" he said. "A real gentleman, made by me! You're going to have everything a London gentleman should have, a carriage, and horses, and everything!" He threw a great thick wallet on to the table. "All that is yours. I've come back to England to watch you spend it."

"Stop!" I cried desperately. "We must discuss your plans. How long are you going to stay here?"

"How long?" he repeated, surprised. "I'm not going back."

"But where will you be safe?"

"Dear boy, who knows I'm here? You, Jaggers, and Wemmick, that's all. Anyway, I know I can live with the fear of death. I've done that all my life."

All I knew was that I must keep him out of sight until Herbert returned. Then we could produce a better plan for the future. I decided to rent a room for him in a house near ours, where I thought he would be safe for the moment. I bought him different clothes and had his hair cut, but to me he looked just the same, and I lived in constant fear that he would be recognized by someone who had known him in the past.

My unwanted guest and I spent five long days and evenings together, with the wind and rain beating on the windows. Those few days seemed more like a year to me. He slept, or ate, or played cards. Sometimes he listened to me reading, with a proud smile on his face. I could not sleep or eat. I used to watch him sleep, wondering what bloody crimes lay in his past, and knowing that I alone protected him from a horrible death.

I cannot describe my joy when Herbert finally returned. At last I could share my terrible news with my friend. He, too, was shocked to hear that my great expectations came from the prisoner I had helped so long ago, and when I introduced him to our guest, Herbert could hardly hide his dislike.

When we were alone, he said to me, "You look so pale, Handel. This has been a painful time for you."

"Herbert, something must be done. He wants to spend even more on me! He must be stopped!"

"You mean you can't accept any more of his money?"

"How can I? You know he's a criminal! How do I know where his money comes from? And think what I owe him already! I have no way of paying him back. Oh Herbert, if I didn't have you as a friend, I'd be desperate!" I could only just control my tears. Herbert kindly pretended not to notice.

"My dear Handel," he said, "if you want to pay back what you owe him, you could always join my company, Clarrikers. I'm going to be a partner there soon, you know." Poor Herbert! He did not suspect whose money was helping him become a partner.

"But there's another thing," added Herbert. "This man has a fierce and violent character. He's come here with a fixed idea, which he's been looking forward to for half his life. If you destroy his idea, his life will be worthless."

"And he will allow himself to be arrested and hanged," I continued, nodding. "Yes, I've thought that ever since he arrived. If that happened, I'd feel guilty for ever."

"So you cannot destroy his dream *now*. First we must get him out of England, where he risks death every moment. *Then* you will explain that you can't accept his money. I'll help you all the way, trust me." I shook Herbert's hand gratefully.

Next morning after breakfast we asked Magwitch to tell us more about his past life so that we could protect him better.

"You promise to keep it a secret, Pip's friend?" he said to Herbert. "Well I'll put it in a few words. In prison and out of prison. That's been my life, more or less. Don't remember my parents. No idea where I was born. I slept in fields, I stole food, and sometimes I worked. And I grew to be a man. It was about twenty years ago I met Compeyson. I'd kill him now, at once, if I met him! He's the man I was fighting when the soldiers found me on the marshes, Pip. He was handsome and educated, so people thought he was a gentleman and trusted him. I was a partner in his business, and a dirty business it was, too. We persuaded rich people to invest their money with us, we used stolen banknotes, and we wrote false checks. Compeyson was clever, but what a wicked, cold heart he had! He always got the profits but never the blame.

"His former partner, Arthur, lived in Compeyson's house and was very ill. In fact he was dying. He and Compeyson had got a lot of money out of a rich lady some years before, and Arthur kept dreaming of this lady. Late one night he appeared at the sitting-room door, pale and shaking, crying, 'Compeyson, she's there! In my room! All dressed in white, ready for the wedding! She's angry, and she says she wants revenge! You broke her heart, you know you did! And now she says I'm going to die!'

"Compeyson and his wife put Arthur back to bed, but at five o'clock in the morning we heard screams coming from his room, and he died soon after.

"I should have realized it was a mistake getting involved with Compeyson. In the end we were both arrested for several crimes. And what happened? At the trial he lied and lied. *I* was the criminal, in and out of prison all my life, and I got fourteen years on the prison ship. *He* was the gentleman, of good character and with important friends, and he only got seven years."

Magwitch had become very excited and had to breathe deeply to calm himself. "I promised myself I'd smash his handsome face when I saw him on the prison ship. I was just going to when a guard caught hold of me. I managed to escape by diving into the river. That's how I reached the marshes and the churchyard. And then Pip, my boy, you told me Compeyson was on the marshes too. He must have escaped, like me. So I hunted him and smashed his face, and I was going to take him back to the prison ship so that he wouldn't have the pleasure of being free, when the soldiers caught us. Again he was clever. His punishment for escaping was light. But I was brought to trial again and sent to Australia for life."

"Is Compeyson dead?" I asked after a silence.

"Heard no more of him," he said, shaking his head. "But if he's alive, he hopes I'm dead—that's certain!"

Herbert passed me a note he had been writing. It said:

"The name of Miss Havisham's half-brother was Arthur. Compeyson is the man who pretended to be in love with her."

14

Pip Visits Estella and Miss Havisham Again

Before taking Magwitch abroad, I felt I must see both Estella and Miss Havisham. When I visited Estella's London home, I found she had gone to stay with Miss Havisham, and so, leaving Magwitch in Herbert's care, I went by coach to the town I knew so well.

Before walking to Miss Havisham's, I went to the hotel for breakfast. It was an unpleasant shock to discover Bentley Drummle there, but I could imagine his reason for visiting the area. When he noticed me, he immediately called to the waiter, making sure I could hear, "Listen, you! The lady isn't going riding today. And remember, I'm not having dinner here tonight, I'll be at the lady's." And Drummle smiled wickedly at me, knowing that what he said cut me to the heart. He went out, shouting for his horse.

If he had spoken Estella's name, I would have hit him. I was so angry with him and so depressed about my future, that I could not eat the breakfast. Instead I went straight to the old house.

I found Miss Havisham and Estella sitting in the same room, with candles burning as usual.

"Miss Havisham," I said, "I must tell you that I'm as unhappy as you ever wanted me to be. I've discovered who has been paying for my education. Now I know I shall never be rich or important. I cannot tell you any more. It isn't my secret, but another person's." I stopped, considering what to say next.

"Go on," said Miss Havisham, looking interested.

"I thought it was you, Miss Havisham! And you encouraged me in my mistake!"

"Why should I be kind to anybody after all I've suffered!" cried Miss Havisham angrily.

"Yes, you're right," I said quickly, to calm her. "But you also encouraged your relations to think I would inherit some of your fortune."

"Why shouldn't I?" she cried wildly.

"But Matthew Pocket and his son are different. They aren't selfish or greedy; they're generous and honest. I want you to know that."

She looked carefully at me. "What do you want for them?"

"I'm asking for money," I replied, my cheeks red. "I would like you to help my friend Herbert become a partner in his company. I started paying for this myself two years ago—and

I want to keep it a secret from him—but now I find I can't continue the payments. I can't explain why. It's part of the other person's secret."

Miss Havisham looked at the fire and then at me again. "What else?" she asked.

Turning to Estella, I tried to control my trembling voice. "You know I love you, Estella," I said. "I have loved you long and dearly." She shook her head.

"I know, I know I have no hope of ever marrying you, Estella. But I have loved you ever since I first saw you in this house. It was cruel of Miss Havisham to encourage me to hope, but I don't think she meant to be unkind."

"What you say," said Estella very calmly, "doesn't touch my heart. I can't feel love as you do. And I've warned you of this. Haven't I?"

"Yes," I answered miserably, "but I couldn't believe it."

"It's the way I've been brought up."

"Estella, Bentley Drummle is in town here. You go riding with him, don't you? Is he having dinner with you tonight?"

"It is all true," she answered, a little surprised.

"You cannot love him, Estella!" I cried.

"Didn't you listen? I can never love anyone!" And then she added, "But why not tell you the truth? I'm going to marry him."

I covered my face with my hands. After a moment I lifted my head and cried, "Don't throw yourself away on an animal like him! Even if you won't marry *me*, there must be others who love you. Any of them would be a thousand times better than Drummle!"

"I can't marry a man who expects me to love him. So Drummle will do well enough as my husband. You will soon forget me."

"Never, Estella! You are part of myself. You are in every line

I've read, in every view I've seen, in every dream I've dreamed. To the last hour of my life, you will remain part of me. God bless you, and God forgive you!" I held her hand to my lips for a moment. As I left, Estella's lovely face looked at me in wonder, but Miss Havisham was staring at me with a mixture of pity and guilt.

It was all over. To calm my feelings I walked all the way back to London. At night the Temple gates were always closed, but the night-porter let me in when I told him my name. He gave me an envelope addressed to Mr. Pip. Inside, in Wemmick's writing, it said: "DON'T GO HOME."

15

Shelter for Magwitch

I spent a restless night at a hotel, worrying about the reasons for Wemmick's warning. Early in the morning I went to see him at the Castle. He told me he had heard I was being watched and that someone was looking for Magwitch. He also knew that Compeyson was alive and in London. While I was absent, Wemmick had warned Herbert to move our guest to a safer place. Clara, the girl Herbert was in love with, lived with her old father in a house on the river, quite near the open sea, and Herbert had arranged to rent rooms for Magwitch in this house. It was further away from the center of London and our home, and we could easily take Magwitch abroad by boat from there.

"Our friend is there now," said Wemmick, "and you can visit him tonight, but don't go back there after that. And remember, Mr. Pip," he added firmly, "remember to get his cash. You don't know what may happen to him. Don't let anything happen to his cash."

I could not explain to Wemmick how I felt about Magwitch's money, so I said nothing.

That evening I visited the house and met Clara, a lovely girl, obviously in love with Herbert. How lucky she and Herbert were! I thought of Estella and felt very sad.

Magwitch seemed quieter and more likeable than the last time I had seen him. He accepted all our arrangements for him gratefully. I was almost sorry to say goodbye to him.

I decided to keep a rowing boat near our rooms, so that Herbert or I could row up and down the river, as far as Clara's house. If Magwitch saw us on the river, he could draw his bedroom curtain to show everything was all right.

For the next few weeks, life went on as normal. Herbert went to work and visited Clara in the evenings. I rowed on the river and waited for news from Wemmick.

One evening, instead of reading alone in my room, I went to the theater where Mr. Wopsle was acting. He noticed me in the audience, and kept looking at me in a very strange way. After the play we met outside the theater, and he asked immediately,

"You didn't see that man sitting right behind you, Mr. Pip?"

I felt suddenly cold. "Who was he?" I asked.

"You remember, Mr. Pip, that Christmas Day, when you were a boy? We went on to the marshes with the soldiers and found the escaped convicts fighting each other. Well, one of those two was looking over your shoulder tonight."

"Which one?" I asked, holding my breath.

"The one with the bleeding face," he answered.

So Compeyson was still following me! I knew Magwitch was in great danger. Later that evening Herbert and I discussed the problem and promised each other to be more careful than ever.

About a week later I met Mr. Jaggers by chance in the street, and he invited me to dinner that evening. Wemmick was there too. Mr. Jaggers told me Miss Havisham wished to see me on business, so I said I would go the next day.

Then Jaggers said, "Well, Pip! Our friend Drummle has won a great prize! He has married Estella!"

I had been expecting this news for some time, but it still came as a terrible shock.

"I wonder," continued Jaggers, "who will be the stronger in the end, the wife or the husband? He may beat her—"

"Surely he isn't wicked enough to do that!" I cried.

"He may, or he may not. But she is certainly more intelligent than him. We shall see."

Just then I noticed the housekeeper putting a dish on the table. I stared at her. I had seen exactly such eyes and such hands, very recently! And suddenly I was absolutely certain that this woman was Estella's mother.

Later, as Wemmick and I left Jaggers' house together, I asked him about his employer's housekeeper. He told me that, many years before, she had been jealous of her husband and another woman and had been accused of murdering this woman. Jaggers was her lawyer, and at her trial he managed to show that she was not strong enough to kill anyone. She was also suspected of killing her three-year-old daughter, who had disappeared. But because of Jaggers' clever arguing, she was judged innocent of murder. After the trial she left her husband and became Jaggers' housekeeper.

16

Miss Havisham Realizes How Pip Has Suffered

When I went to see Miss Havisham the next day as she had requested, her house looked darker than ever, and I realized how lonely she was without Estella. She looked sadly at me.

"Tell me, Pip," she said, stretching out her hand to me, "how can I help your friend? You said something about it last time."

I explained my agreement with Clarrikers to make Herbert a partner. Nine hundred pounds still had to be paid.

"And you will be happier if I pay this?"

"Much happier."

"Can't I help you yourself, Pip?"

"There is nothing you can do," I answered.

She wrote a check, which she handed to me. "Mr. Jaggers will give you the money. And—here, Pip," handing me another piece of paper, "here is a note with my name on. If, one day, you can write under my name 'I forgive her', please do it."

"Oh Miss Havisham," I said, "I can do it now. We have all made mistakes. I can't be bitter with anyone."

"What have I done, Pip!" she cried, dropping to her knees in front of me. "I should never have brought up Estella like that or allowed you to be hurt!"

"Could I ask you something about Estella? How and why did you adopt her?"

"I never knew her parents," she said quietly. "I asked Jaggers to find a little girl for me to adopt, and he brought Estella here when she was about three."

We had no more to say to each other, and so I left. But on my way through the old garden I had a strange feeling that something was wrong, and I ran back upstairs to check that Miss Havisham was all right. As I opened the door of her room, I saw her sitting close to the fire. Suddenly a great flame lit the room. She turned and rushed towards me, screaming, her hair and clothes on fire. Somehow I managed to cover her with my coat and put out the flames with my hands.

Suddenly a great flame lit the room.

I sent for a doctor, who cleaned her wounds. Her bed was placed on the great dining table, where her wedding cake had been, and she lay there, covered with a white sheet, half conscious. I could not stay, but left her in the care of the doctor and several nurses and returned to London.

My hands and right arm had been badly burned. But although I was in great pain, I was desperate to know if Magwitch was safe.

"Everything's fine, Handel," Herbert told me calmly, as he gently put bandages on my hands. "He seems much pleasanter than before. I actually like him now. Do you know, yesterday he was telling me about his past. Apparently at one time he was married to a young woman who was jealous of another woman. There was a fight, and his wife killed the other. Luckily for her, she had a clever lawyer at her trial and was never punished for the murder. She and Magwitch had a daughter, who Magwitch dearly loved. Both wife and child disappeared after the trial, and he thought his wife must have killed their daughter."

"How old was the child?" I asked, trying to control my excitement.

"She would have been about your age if she had lived."

"Herbert," I said, "am I ill or mad or anything?"

"No," replied Herbert, after examining me carefully, "although you do look a little excited."

"Listen, Herbert. Magwitch is Estella's father."

The next day, although I felt ill and weak because of my burns, I went straight to Jaggers' office. He admitted that Estella was his housekeeper's daughter, adopted by Miss Havisham to give her the chance of a better life. But even he, the great Jaggers, did not know that Magwitch was Estella's father.

17

Pip Is Close to Death

I paid Clarrikers Miss Havisham's nine hundred pounds and felt glad that Herbert's future, at least, was safe. Clarrikers were going to send Herbert to India to open a new office there. So while helping my old friend, I would be losing him at the same time.

Wemmick advised us to move Magwitch out of the country in the middle of the week. So we decided to row the boat down to Clara's house on Wednesday, collect Magwitch, and continue right down the river to Essex, where we could stop one of the foreign ships sailing from the port of London to Germany or Holland. With luck, nobody would notice us or suspect us. Our friend Startop agreed to row instead of me, as my hands were still too painful.

However, when I went back to our rooms on Monday, my head full of arrangements for the journey, I found a letter, addressed to me, and delivered by hand. It said:

"If you want information about *your guest*, you should come tonight or tomorrow night to the old house near the lime-kiln on the marshes, Tell no one. *You must come alone*."

I did not have time to consider. I rushed out again and was just in time to catch the afternoon coach.

I stopped in town only to ask about Miss Havisham. She was still very ill, it seemed. Then I walked fast on to the dark lonely marshes. Soon I arrived at the lime-kiln, which was still burning, although the workmen had all gone home. I pushed open the door of the old house, which I thought was uninhabited, but to my surprise there was a bed, a table, and a candle inside. Suddenly the candle was blown out, I was attacked from behind, and my arms were tied close to my sides with a thick rope. The pain in my injured arm was terrible. In a moment the candle was lit again, and I recognized my attacker. Orlick! I saw he had been drinking, and I knew I was in a very dangerous situation.

"Now," he said fiercely, "I've got you!"

"Why have you brought me here?" I asked.

"Don't you know?" he replied, drinking straight from a bottle. "Because you're my enemy. I lost that job at Miss Havisham's because of you. And what's more, Biddy would have liked me if *you* hadn't been there. You've been in my way ever since you were a child. And now I'm going to have your life! Tonight you're going to die!"

I felt I was looking down into my own grave. I could see no possible way of escape.

"Tonight you're going to die!"

"More than that," he said, "I don't want anything left of you. I'll put your body in the kiln. Even your clothes will be burned, and in the morning there'll be nothing left."

I realized I had not told anybody where I was going. Nobody would know where to look for me.

"Another thing," he said, smiling cruelly, "it was your fault your ugly sister was attacked. I did it, I hit her with the iron chain your convict left on the marshes, but I did it because I hated *you*!" He drank again. I watched the level of the liquid go down. I knew that when he finished the bottle, my life would end.

"And I know all about that convict you're hiding. I've waited and watched outside your rooms and on the stairs. You fell over me once. I've got a friend who's going to inform the police about him. Yes, Compeyson'll make sure he's hanged, when you're dead!"

The last of the rum went down his throat, and picking up his hammer he came towards me. Determined to fight, I shouted as loudly as I could. Suddenly the door was thrown open, and Herbert and Startop rushed in. With a violent shout Orlick jumped over the table and escaped into the night.

My two friends had found Orlick's letter to me, which, in my hurry, I had dropped in my room in London. They had suspected some wicked plot and come straight to the town, and then to the marshes, to find me. Luckily they had arrived just in time.

They took me back to London that night and looked after me carefully all the next day, so that, although my arm was still aching, and I felt very weak, I was fit enough for the planned journey on Wednesday.

18

The End of Magwitch's Story

It was a cold, bright morning when we set out cheerfully down the river. I steered the boat, and Herbert and Startop rowed. At Clara's house Magwitch was waiting for us, wrapped in a dark cloak.

"Dear boy!" he said, putting his hand on my shoulder as he sat down heavily in the boat. "Thank you!"

We rowed eastwards down the river all day, looking around all the time to check that no one was following us. Magwitch seemed quite happy, smoking his pipe and watching the water.

"You don't know what a pleasure it is to me, Pip," he said once, "to be with my dear boy, in the open air."

"You'll be completely safe, and free tomorrow," I said.

"I hope so, dear boy. But looking into the future, well, that's like looking for the bottom of the river, isn't it? Can't be done." He remained silent after that.

We decided to spend the night at a little riverside pub. It seemed safe because there were no other guests, but the pub owner asked us a question which worried us.

"Did you see that boat go past, gentlemen? Rowed by four men, with two others on board. It's been up and down the river several times. Could be a Customs boat."

When he left us alone, we discussed this information in whispers. In the end we decided to go to bed and then set out the next morning just in time to catch the ship to Hamburg. I woke early, and when I looked out of the window, I saw two men examining our boat, but I decided not to wake Herbert or Startop, who needed their rest after rowing all the previous day.

Late in the morning we rowed into the center of the river.

We could see the ship to Hamburg coming closer. Magwitch and I picked up our bags and said goodbye to Herbert and Startop so that we would be ready to stop the ship and get on board. Suddenly a boat rowed by four men appeared from nowhere and came out very fast into the center of the river, close to us. A fifth man was steering, and a sixth, his face hidden in his cloak, whispered instructions to the steerer. They all stared at us.

"You have a convict there who's returned from Australia," shouted the steerer. "That's the man, in the cloak. His name is Abel Magwitch. I'm a Customs officer, and I arrest him!"

Suddenly their boat was touching ours. The Hamburg ship was almost on top of us, and the ship's captain shouted the order to stop engines, but it was too late. At the same moment the Customs officer put his hand on Magwitch's shoulder, and Magwitch pulled the cloak off the other man in the boat. It was Compeyson! And as I watched, he fell backwards into the water, his face full of terror. The huge ship hit our tiny boat with a great crash. Somehow the Customs officers managed to get me on board their boat, with Herbert and Startop, but our boat sank, and the two convicts had disappeared.

Soon, however, we discovered Magwitch in the water, badly injured, and pulled him into the boat. He told me that he had fallen into the water with Compeyson, and then been hit by the ship. I believed what he said. At the time there was no sign of Compeyson, whose dead body was found several days later.

Magwitch was taken to prison to wait for his trial. I arranged for Jaggers to be his lawyer, but Jaggers warned me there was almost no hope of saving his life. Magwitch's thick wallet was handed over to the police, and Wemmick was quite annoyed with me about it.

"Really, Mr. Pip, to lose so much cash!" he said. "You see,

The huge ship hit our tiny boat with a great crash.

Compeyson was so determined to get his revenge that you couldn't have saved Magwitch. But you certainly *could* have saved the cash. That's the difference. But could I ask you something, Mr. Pip? Would you come for a walk with me on Monday morning?"

It seemed a strange request, and although I did not really feel like accepting, he politely insisted.

I arrived at the Castle early on Monday morning, and after a glass of rum and milk, we set out on the road.

"Well, well!" said Wemmick suddenly. "Here's a church! Let's go in!" And when we were inside, there was another surprise.

"Well, well!" he said again. "Look what I've found in my pockets! Let's put them on!" As he had "found" two pairs of white gloves and his post-box mouth was as wide as it could possibly be, I began to suspect something. And when I saw the Aged come in with a lady, I knew I was right.

"Well, well!" said Wemmick, still pretending to be surprised, "here's the Aged and Miss Skiffins! Let's have a wedding!"

And so Wemmick was married to Miss Skiffins, and we all celebrated afterwards at a little pub near the church.

I was delighted for Wemmick, but I could not stop worrying about Magwitch. He had been so badly injured that he was moved to the prison hospital, where I visited him every day. I read to him, talked to him, and did everything I could to make him comfortable. But day by day I watched him becoming weaker although he never complained. To the prison guards he was a dangerous criminal, but to me he was an unfortunate man, who had at least some goodness in him. I could not leave him now.

At his trial Jaggers was proved right. The judge decided that Magwitch, a convict sent away for life who had returned, must be hanged. I could not accept this terrible punishment and wrote to all the important people I could think of, asking for mercy for Magwitch. But all of them refused to help.

I noticed, on my daily visits to him, that he was getting much worse. He lay in bed, looking calmly at the white ceiling. Sometimes he could not speak and just pressed my hand. One evening as I entered his room, he smiled weakly at me.

"Dear boy," he said, "you're never late."

"I don't want to lose a moment of the time I'm allowed to visit you," I said.

"Thank you, dear boy. God bless you! You've never deserted me, dear boy!" He had spoken his last words.

I touched his chest, remembering that I had wanted to desert him once. He put both his hands on mine.

"Dear Magwitch, listen to me. You had a child once, who you loved and lost." He pressed my hand gently. "She's alive. She's a lady and very beautiful. And I love her!"

He was too weak to speak any more, but he just managed to lift my hand to his lips. Then he looked peacefully up at the white ceiling again. Slowly his eyes closed, and his head dropped quietly on to his chest.

19

A Wedding

The excitement of all these events made me seriously ill for several weeks. Herbert was abroad, on business for Clarrikers, and there would have been nobody to look after me, if Joe had not heard about my illness and come to London to nurse me.

When I was getting better, he told me some of the local news. Miss Havisham had died and left all her fortune to Estella, except for £4000, which Matthew Pocket inherited. And Orlick had been arrested for breaking into Pumblechook's house and stealing his money. Dear old Joe seemed just the same, but as I got better, he began to remember I was a gentleman and call me sir again, and when I got up one morning, I discovered he had gone.

I decided to go back to the village to thank him for all his help and to carry out a plan I had been considering for some time. I wanted to ask Biddy to marry me, and I knew I would be happy with her. So I went by coach to the old town, as I had done so many times before, and walked to the forge. But as I came closer, I could not hear the sound of Joe's hammer, and I noticed fresh white curtains at the windows, and bright flowers everywhere. Suddenly I saw Biddy and Joe at the door, arm in arm.

"Pip!" cried Biddy happily, running to kiss me. "Pip, it's my wedding day, and I'm married to Joe!"

I was still weak from my illness, and the shock was too much for me. They had to help me into the house and let me rest in a chair. They were both so pleased that I had come, by accident, to make their day perfect. I could only be glad that I had never spoken of my plan to Joe when he was looking after me.

"Dear Biddy," I said, "you have the best husband in the whole world."

"I couldn't love him more than I do," she replied.

"And dear Joe, you have the best wife in the world, and she will make you as happy as even you deserve to be, dear good Joe!" Joe put his arm over his eyes. "And Joe and Biddy, I want to thank you from the bottom of my heart for all you've done for me. Tell me you forgive me for not being grateful and not being good. And think better of me in the future!"

"Oh dear old Pip," said Joe, "God knows we forgive you, if there is anything to forgive!"

So I left the forge and started a new life, working as a clerk for Clarrikers, Herbert's company. I was sent to the new office in India to take charge, while Herbert came back to England to marry his Clara.

Herbert and his wife invited me to live with them, and we all stayed out in India for many years. In the end, I too became a partner in the company. We worked hard and honestly, and we made good profits.

It was not until eleven years later that I returned to England and saw Biddy and Joe again although I had been writing regularly to them. One evening in December I gently pushed open the old kitchen door, and there, sitting by the fire next to Joe, in my old place, was—Pip! Joe and Biddy's son had my name and looked just like me. They also had a little daughter and were the happiest of parents.

"Dear Pip," said Biddy quietly to me after supper, "have you quite forgotten *her*? Tell me, as an old friend."

"My dear Biddy, I can never forget her. But that was all a dream, which has passed!"

But I was secretly planning to revisit Miss Havisham's old house, alone, as a way of remembering Estella. I had heard that her husband had been very cruel to her. They had separated, and then he had died two years ago. Perhaps she had remarried by now.

The old house had been knocked down, and there was nothing left but piles of stones in the garden. In the moonlight I walked sadly around until suddenly I saw a woman's figure in the shadows. I went closer and then—

"Estella!" I cried.

"You recognize me? I have changed a lot," she answered.

She was older, but still beautiful. I had never before seen such a soft light in those once proud eyes or felt such a friendly touch of her once cold hand.

"It's strange, Estella! After so many years, we meet by chance, here, where we first met!"

"Yes, it's strange. I haven't been here for years, although the land belongs to me. But tell me, you still live abroad?"

"Yes, I still do. I'm doing well in India."

"I've often thought of you. Since—my husband—died, I have given you a place in my heart."

"You have always held *your* place in *my* heart," I answered.

There was silence for a few moments.

"I didn't think I would say goodbye to you here," she said.

"It's painful saying goodbye, Estella."

"But last time you said, 'God bless you, and God forgive you!' You could say that to me now, now that I understand how much you loved me, now that I have suffered, and now that I am a better person. Tell me we are friends." She spoke more eagerly than I had ever heard her speak before.

"We are friends," I said, taking her hand.

"And will continue being friends, even when we are apart," said Estella,

We walked, hand in hand, out of the old garden. As the morning mist had risen long ago when I first left the forge, so the evening mist was rising now, and in the clear moonlight I saw no shadow of another separation from her.

GLOSSARY

abroad in or to another country
admire to look at with pleasure, to like; **admiration** (*n*)
apprentice (*n*) a young person who learns his/her job by working with an experienced workman
aged old ("aged parent" is Wemmick's name for his father)
blacksmith someone whose job is to make and repair things made of iron
bless to ask God to protect and look after someone
on board on a boat or ship
brandy a strong alcoholic drink
candle a round stick of wax which burns to give light
carriage a coach pulled by horses
chain a line of heavy iron rings attached to a prisoner to prevent him from escaping
cheek the side of your face
churchyard ground near a church where dead people are buried
client a customer
cloak a sleeveless coat that hangs loosely from the shoulders
common uneducated; regarded as belonging to a low social class
convict a criminal who has been found guilty of a crime and sent to prison
counting-house a company whose business is checking profits and payments for other companies
deserve to be good enough or worthy enough for something
disgust (*n*) a strong feeling of dislike
dramatic (*adj*) done in a sudden, exciting, or impressive way, for special effect
expectation something expected; a belief that something will happen

file (*n*) a metal tool with a rough surface for cutting or smoothing things

firmly in a strong and determined way

forge a place, used by a blacksmith, where metals are heated and shaped

gentleman a man of good family, usually wealthy

gravy a thick sauce poured over meat

handcuffs metal bracelets used by the police when arresting or moving criminals

hang to kill someone by hanging them from a rope around the neck

housekeeper a person employed to manage a house

impression an appearance or effect that may be false

improve to get better, or to make something better

insure to pay money to an insurance company, which promises to pay you in case of accident, injury, damage, etc.

invest to put money into a bank or business

lime-kiln an oven which burns to produce lime (lime is used for building and on farms)

marsh low, flat, wet ground

master a man who employs others or has an apprentice

nod (*v*) to move your head up and down in agreement

opportunity a chance; the right moment

pale having little color (e.g., in the face)

partner a person who works with another in a shared business

pie a fruit or meat dish, which can be eaten hot or cold

roast (*v*) to cook meat in the oven

rum a strong alcoholic drink, often drunk hot

scold (*v*) to speak angrily to someone because they have done something wrong

sink (past tense **sank**) to go down and disappear under water

smash (*v*) to break, or be broken, violently and noisily
the Temple an area of London
trust (*v*) to have confidence in someone
wicked of bad character

ACTIVITIES

Before Reading

1 **Read the story introduction on the first page of the book and the back cover. What do you know about the story now? Circle Y (Yes) or N (No) for each of the statements.**

1 Miss Havisham's wedding was cancelled. Y/N
2 Miss Havisham wants Pip to fall in love. Y/N
3 Estella is one of Pip's friends. Y/N
4 Pip comes from a well-educated country family. Y/N
5 Pip is happy until he hears about his "great expectations." Y/N

2 **What do you think Pip's "great expectations" will be? Choose one or more of these possibilities.**

1 His education will be paid for.
2 He will be trained for a profession.
3 A marriage will be arranged between him and a lady of high social position.
4 He will be given an easy job with a high salary.
5 He will inherit a fortune.

3 **What do you think is going to happen in the story? Can you guess the answers to these questions?**

1 Will Pip and Estella marry, and if so, will they be happy?
2 Will Miss Havisham help Pip to move upwards in society?
3 Will Pip be disappointed by his "great expectations" in the end?
4 Will Pip's "great expectations" ruin his life?
5 Will Pip be successful in life without anybody's help?

ACTIVITIES

While Reading

Read Chapters 1 to 3, and answer these questions.

1 Why did Pip often visit the churchyard?
2 What did Pip think "bringing up by hand" meant?
3 What did Pip steal from the kitchen for the convict?
4 Why did the convict need the file?
5 Why did the convict tell the soldiers he had stolen food from the blacksmith's house?
6 What happened to the two escaped convicts?
7 Why did Miss Havisham invite Pip to her house?
8 What was strange about Miss Havisham?
9 How did Pip feel about Estella?
10 Why did Pip lie to his family about his visit to Miss Havisham?

Read Chapters 4 to 6. Who said this to whom, and who or what were they talking about?

1 "I'd like to give the boy something."
2 "I'll never cry for you again."
3 "This is where they will put me when I'm dead."
4 "I want my revenge!"
5 "Well, here you are—it's twenty-five pounds!"
6 "Something wrong up at the forge!"
7 "Don't you think you're happier as you are?"
8 "I'd never stand in Pip's way, never."
9 "Do you accept these conditions?"
10 "This is a bad side of your character."

Before you read Chapters 7 to 11, can you guess what happens? Circle Y (Yes) or N (No) for each of these ideas.

1 Pip has difficulty in getting used to London. Y/N
2 He makes some good friends in London. Y/N
3 He learns Miss Havisham's history. Y/N
4 He often goes home to visit Joe and Biddy. Y/N
5 Pip realizes he loves Biddy, not Estella. Y/N

Read Chapters 7 to 11. Are these sentences true (T) or false (F)? Rewrite the false sentences with the correct information.

1 Pip's first impression of London was disappointing.
2 Herbert Pocket thought Estella was a lovely girl, and he wanted to marry her himself.
3 Wemmick lived in a castle in London.
4 Mr. Jaggers was often robbed because he left his doors unlocked.
5 Pip was ashamed of Joe when Joe came to see him in London.
6 Magwitch was a friend of Pip's.
7 Estella told Pip that she loved him.
8 Herbert planned to marry Clara for her money.
9 Herbert advised Pip to forget Estella.
10 Pip promised to visit Joe more often, and Biddy believed him.

Before you read Chapter 12 (*Pip Discovers the Truth*), what do you think the truth might be? Choose one of these ideas.

1 Pip will discover his money has come from Miss Havisham.
2 He will learn that the money has come from someone else.
3 He will learn that Herbert is secretly engaged to Estella.
4 He will learn that the money has all gone and that he no longer has "great expectations."

Read Chapters 12 to 15. Choose the best question-word for these questions and then answer them.

Why / Who / What

1 . . . followed Estella everywhere?
2 . . . had paid for Pip's education and all his living expenses?
3 . . . would happen if the police discovered Magwitch had returned to England?
4 . . . was Pip so upset when he discovered the truth?
5 . . . did Magwitch hate Compeyson so much?
6 . . . was the connection between Magwitch and Miss Havisham?
7 . . . did Pip ask Miss Havisham for money?
8 . . . did Estella agree to marry Bentley Drummle?
9 . . . warned Pip not to go home?
10 . . . was Magwitch moved to rooms in Clara's father's house?
11 . . . did Pip find out when he went to the theater one night?
12 . . . was Estella's mother?

Before you read Chapters 16 to 19, can you guess how the story ends? Circle Y (Yes) or N (No) for each possibility.

1 Pip discovers that Mr. Jaggers is Estella's father. Y/N
2 Miss Havisham asks Pip to forgive her. Y/N
3 Miss Havisham dies and leaves all her money to Pip. Y/N
4 Pip earns enough money to go on living as a gentleman. Y/N
5 Herbert makes a lot of money and helps Pip find a job. Y/N
6 The police arrest Magwitch, and he is sent for trial. Y/N
7 Pip inherits Magwitch's fortune and marries Biddy. Y/N
8 Estella kills her husband and goes to live with her mother. Y/N
9 Estella tells Pip she has given him a place in her heart. Y/N

ACTIVITIES

After Reading

1 **What happened to Magwitch in the end? Match these parts of sentences, and use the linking words to make a paragraph of seven sentences. Start with number 3.**

and / and / and although / before / but / but / however / in order to / that / which / while / who

1 _____ they were waiting for the Hamburg ship to reach them,
2 Magwitch was soon rescued, alive but badly injured,
3 Pip and his friends rowed Magwitch down the River Thames,
4 The Customs officer tried to arrest Magwitch,
5 _____, Magwitch died in his bed in the prison hospital
6 The Hamburg ship then crashed into Pip's boat,
7 At Magwitch's trial the judge decided
8 _____ catch the ship to Hamburg.
9 a Customs boat suddenly appeared from nowhere
10 _____ Magwitch fell into the river with Compeyson,
11 _____ sank,
12 _____ Compeyson's body was not found until some days later.
13 _____ Magwitch must be hanged,
14 everybody refused to help him.
15 _____ came up close to Pip's rowing-boat.
16 _____ had been hidden under a cloak in the Customs boat.
17 _____ in the confusion the two convicts disappeared.
18 _____ Pip tried very hard to get this punishment changed,
19 _____ this terrible punishment could take place.

2 **Who's who in this story? Match these names with the information about them.**

Mrs. Joe Gargery	Magwitch	Miss Havisham
Joe Gargery	Biddy	Mr. Jaggers
Mr. Pumblechook	Estella	Wemmick
Herbert Pocket		

1 . . . thought Pip was a common working boy and laughed at him.
2 . . . brought Pip up "by hand" and often scolded him.
3 . . . used to wash away his clients and his work every evening before leaving the office.
4 . . . was looking about him for a good opportunity of making his fortune in the City.
5 . . . encouraged Estella to break Pip's heart.
6 . . . never spoke of the Castle at the office and never thought about the office at the Castle.
7 . . . refused Pip's request to teach Joe better manners because she thought Joe's manners were fine as they were.
8 . . . comforted Pip whenever he could and tried to protect him from being punished.
9 . . . was Estella's father, but he thought she had died many years ago.
10 . . . was hoping to find a young gentleman who would put money into his business.

What did these people have to do with Pip? How did they influence his life? Write a short paragraph about each of them, using the sentences above and other information from the story.

3 What was Magwitch thinking, on that early morning on the marshes, just after Pip had brought him the food and run away? Choose one suitable word to fill each gap.

This is a good, strong blacksmith's _____. I'm nearly through the chain already, _____ then I'll be able to walk _____. Lucky finding that boy in the _____! Poor little boy! He looked so _____ when I jumped up from the _____ and caught hold of him. I _____ have looked very fierce. I was _____ for food! Pity I had to _____ him a bit, but I didn't _____ him at all. I wanted to _____ quite sure he would keep my _____. Sad really—says he's lost his _____. Buried in the churchyard, they are.

_____, he's brought me the food I _____. That sister of his is a _____ cook. I've eaten all the meat _____, the bread, and cheese, and I've _____ the brandy. I feel a lot _____ now. I hadn't had a thing _____ eat since I escaped. I must _____ the boy's name—Pip. Wish I _____ a son like him. Maybe one _____ I can find a way of _____ him for helping me.

And because _____ him, I now know I'm not _____ only escaped convict out on the _____. Someone must have got away last _____. The boy said it was a _____ man, and I think it's that _____ Compeyson! At last! This is my _____ to finish with him! If this _____ weren't so thick, I could find _____ at once and smash his handsome, _____ face! But as soon as it's _____, I'll search the marshes, and when _____ catch up with him, he'll be _____ he tricked me! I don't care _____ they catch me as long as _____ catch him as well. Death would _____ too easy, too quick a punishment _____ him. I want to see him _____ on that prison ship for years and _____!

4 How did Pip learn who Estella's parents were? (See pages 72 and 75.) Complete Pip's side of these two conversations.

PIP: How long has Mr. Jaggers' housekeeper worked for him?
WEMMICK: Molly? Oh, for years. Ever since her trial, in fact.
PIP: __________
WEMMICK: Murder, Mr. Pip. She was jealous of her husband and another woman, and she was accused of murdering this woman.
PIP: __________
WEMMICK: No, innocent. The case against her wasn't proved. Mr. Jaggers was her lawyer, you see, and he's a clever man.
PIP: __________
WEMMICK: Yes, a three-year-old girl, who disappeared at the time of the murder. Molly was accused of murdering her too, but it wasn't proved. But how did you know about the daughter?
PIP: __________

• • •

MR. JAGGERS: Yes, Mr. Pip, what can I do for you?
PIP: __________
MR. JAGGERS: How do you know my housekeeper has a daughter?
PIP: __________
MR. JAGGERS: Well, yes, you're right. It is Estella. She was adopted by Miss Havisham when she was three.
PIP: __________
MR. JAGGERS: Because she wanted the child to have the chance of a better life. And Miss Havisham wanted to adopt a girl, so . . .
PIP: __________
MR. JAGGERS: No, I don't. Why? Do *you* know who he is?
PIP: __________
MR. JAGGERS: Well, well, well. And are you going to tell Estella?
PIP: __________

5 Do you agree (A) or disagree (D) with these statements about the characters? Explain why.

1. Joe should not have allowed his wife to scold him and give him orders, or to beat Pip with a stick.
2. Mr. Pumblechook was an honest, sincere man who only had Pip's best interests at heart.
3. Miss Havisham was right to use Estella to take her revenge on men.
4. Biddy understood Pip better than anyone else in the story.
5. Compeyson was not as wicked as Orlick.
6. Mr. Jaggers was only interested in finding the truth and in making sure that the guilty were punished.
7. Pip needed Herbert Pocket more than Herbert needed Pip.
8. If Magwitch's marriage had not broken up, he would not have become a criminal.

6 How did these people's characters develop and improve during the story? What caused them to change?

Mrs. Joe Gargery / Pip / Estella / Miss Havisham / Abel Magwitch

7 Did you like the ending of the story, or would you have preferred a different one? Choose from these ideas, or use one of your own, and write a new ending for the story.

1. Pip meets Estella again at the old house, but she is still as cold and distant as ever, and they say goodbye for the last time.
2. Pip never sees Estella again and remains single all his life.
3. Joe dies. Pip marries Biddy and becomes a good father to Joe's children.

ABOUT THE AUTHOR

Charles John Huffam Dickens (1812—70) was born in Portsmouth, a port in the south of England. His father was a clerk in the Royal Navy pay office, a well-meaning but irresponsible man, and very bad at managing money. Dickens spent some happy childhood years in Kent, but when the family moved to London, their money problems resulted in his father's imprisonment for debt in the Marshalsea prison, and at the age of twelve Dickens was sent to work in a factory. Bitter memories of this deeply unhappy time influenced much of his writing. Later, he was able to return to school for a few years, and after a time as an office boy, he became a journalist, writing for various newspapers. In these early years Dickens got to know London extremely well—all its highways and passages, its squares, markets, and gardens—and this was knowledge that he put to very good use in his novels.

In 1836 he married Catherine Hogarth, and in the same year his first novel, *The Pickwick Papers*, began to appear in monthly installments in a magazine. This was very popular, and it was soon followed by *Oliver Twist* and several more novels. They were all written as serials for monthly magazines and published as books later. Readers eagerly greeted each new novel, and Dickens quickly became both successful and wealthy.

As well as his writing, Dickens found time for a busy social life with his large family and wide circle of friends, for his theatrical activities, for editing magazines, and for traveling in America and Europe. He also had a great interest in the social problems of the times—a concern that appears in many of his novels. For example, in his famous story *A Christmas Carol*

(1843), Scrooge is shown as mean and hard-hearted because he refuses to give money to the hungry and the homeless.

As he grew older, Dickens worked harder than ever, and the novels of these later years—*Dombey and Son, David Copperfield, Bleak House, Hard Times, Little Dorrit, A Tale of Two Cities, Great Expectations*—are often considered to be his finest works. His personal life, though, became rather difficult, and his marriage came to an end when he and Catherine separated in 1858. The novels, however, continued to appear, and Dickens toured Britain and the United States, giving public readings from his works. It was a very full but also exhausting life, and in 1870, at the age of 58, Dickens died suddenly, leaving unfinished his last novel, *The Mystery of Edwin Drood*.

Great Expectations, published in 1861, has all the usual "Dickensian" richness and variety: amusing minor characters, such as Pumblechook and Wemmick, with his "aged parent"; a complicated plot full of surprises; and the human values painfully learned by Pip as he passes through the various stages of his "great expectations." In the original ending, Pip and Estella remain apart, but Dickens was advised to change this to the happy ending expected by the reading public. Films of this popular novel include the famous David Lean film of 1946, and a 1998 version, set in modern Florida and New York.

Many books have been written about the life and works of Charles Dickens, and there have been many film, stage, and musical adaptations of his stories. He is often called the greatest English novelist of all time, and his characters and their sayings have become so real to us that they are now part of our language and our everyday life.

OXFORD BOOKWORMS LIBRARY

Classics • Crime & Mystery • Factfiles • Fantasy & Horror
Human Interest • Playscripts • Thriller & Adventure
True Stories • World Stories

The OXFORD BOOKWORMS LIBRARY provides enjoyable reading in English, with a wide range of classic and modern fiction, non-fiction, and plays. It includes original and adapted texts in seven carefully graded language stages which take learners from beginner to advanced level.

All Stage 1 titles, as well as over eighty other titles from Starter to Stage 6, are available as audio recordings. All Starters and many titles at Stages 1 to 4 are specially recommended for younger learners. Every Bookworm is illustrated, and Starters and Factfiles have full-color illustrations.

The OXFORD BOOKWORMS LIBRARY also offers extensive support. Each book contains an introduction to the story, notes about the author, a glossary, and activities. Additional resources include tests and worksheets, as well as answers for these and for the activities in the books. There is advice on running a class library, using audio recordings, and the many ways of using Oxford Bookworms in reading programs. Resource materials are available on the website <www.oup.com/elt/gradedreaders>.

The *Oxford Bookworms Collection* is a series for advanced learners. It consists of volumes of short stories by well-known authors, both classic and modern. Texts are not abridged or adapted in any way, but carefully selected to be accessible to the advanced student.

You can find details and a full list of titles in the *Oxford Bookworms Library Catalog* and *Oxford English Language Teaching Catalogs*, and on the website <www.oup.com/elt/gradedreaders>.

BOOKWORMS · CLASSICS · STAGE 4

A Tale of Two Cities

CHARLES DICKENS

Retold by Ralph Mowat

"The Marquis lay there, like stone, with a knife pushed into his heart. On his chest lay a piece of paper, with the words: *Drive him fast to the grave. This is from JACQUES.*"

The French Revolution brings terror and death to many people. But even in these troubled times people can still love and be kind. They can be generous, true-hearted . . . and brave.

BOOKWORMS · HUMAN INTEREST · STAGE 4

Little Women

LOUISA MAY ALCOTT

Retold by John Escott

When Christmas comes for the four March girls, there is no money for expensive presents, and they give away their Christmas breakfast to a poor family. But there are no happier girls in America than Meg, Jo, Beth, and Amy. They miss their father, of course, who is away at the Civil War, but they try hard to be good so that he will be proud of his "little women" when he comes home.

This heart-warming story of family life has been popular for more than a hundred years.

BOOKWORMS · FANTASY & HORROR · STAGE 4

Dr. Jekyll and Mr. Hyde

ROBERT LOUIS STEVENSON

Retold by Rosemary Border

You are walking through the streets of London. It is getting dark, and you want to get home quickly. You enter a narrow side-street. Everything is quiet, but as you pass the door of a large windowless building, you hear a key turning in the lock. A man comes out and looks at you. You have never seen him before, but you realize immediately that he hates you. You are shocked to discover, also, that you hate him.

Who is this man that everybody hates? And why is he coming out of the laboratory of the very respectable Dr. Jekyll?

BOOKWORMS · CLASSICS · STAGE 5

Wuthering Heights

EMILY BRONTË

Retold by Clare West

The wind is strong on the Yorkshire moors. There are few trees and fewer houses to block its path. There is one house, however, that does not hide from the wind. It stands out from the hill and challenges the wind to do its worst. The house is called Wuthering Heights.

When Mr. Earnshaw brings a strange, small, dark child back home to Wuthering Heights, it seems he has opened his doors to trouble. He has invited in something that, like the wind, is safer kept out of the house.

BOOKWORMS · CLASSICS · STAGE 6

Oliver Twist

CHARLES DICKENS

Retold by Richard Rogers

London in the 1830s was no place to be if you were a hungry ten-year-old boy, an orphan without friends or family, with no home to go to, and with only a penny in your pocket to buy a piece of bread.

But Oliver Twist finds some friends—Fagin, the Artful Dodger, and Charley Bates. They give him food and shelter and play games with him, but it is not until some days later that Oliver finds out what kind of friends they are and what kind of "games" they play . . .

BOOKWORMS · CLASSICS · STAGE 6

Pride and Prejudice

JANE AUSTEN

Retold by Clare West

"The moment I first met you, I noticed your pride, your sense of superiority, and your selfish disdain for the feelings of others. You are the last man in the world whom I could ever be persuaded to marry," said Elizabeth Bennet.

And so Elizabeth rejects the proud Mr. Darcy. Can nothing overcome her prejudice against him? And what of the other Bennet girls—their fortunes and misfortunes in the business of getting husbands?

This famous novel by Jane Austen is full of wise and humorous observation of the people and manners of her times.